The Chocolate Gossip Party

1

~THE FaiRY Ring~

Rebecca Carr Schrodt

For my two boys, Andrew and Jordan, who taught me what it means to be a mother and to never let go of your imagination.

For my parents, Dawson and Bobbi, a.k.a., Daddy and Mama, for encouraging me years ago to write a children's book. And for their support and belief in me.

Acknowledgments

Thanks to Josh Tufts for the fantastic book cover and illustrations. You can view his other works at: www.Joshtuftsart.com

Thanks to Ellen Brock my editor for her help and expertise on many aspects of the book. https://ellenbrockediting.com/

Many thanks to my parents, Dawson and Bobbi Carr, and my cousins Janet, Sierra, Devin Bonney and Jayne Sabino for the many hours spent reading and re-reading the book and helping with corrections.

And most of all, thanks to Taylor Robbins who posted on social media one day, "Who wants to come over to eat chocolate and gossip?" That gave me the inspiration to write this story.

www.TheChocolateGossipParty.com

CONTENTS

1

THE Chocolate Gossip Party

Taylor May Dawson fumbled with her locker in the noisy hall of West Corner Middle School. It was the last day of school before summer break and Taylor was looking forward to a summer filled with fun and adventure. She grabbed her lunch and headed down the hall. The latch on her lunchbox broke and out dumped her sandwich, apple, and chips onto the middle of the floor. As Taylor bent down to pick up her lunch, Stephanie, Jennifer and Angela came sauntering out of the cafeteria, arm in arm with noses held high. They lived on the backside of Taylor's neighborhood, McLendon Heights, the rich side, with huge houses and manicured lawns. Taylor called them the Mansion Girls.

The Mansion Girls were snooty, always avoided eye contact with Taylor and never spoke to her, even when they brushed by her in the halls at school. They were seventh graders, a whole grade ahead of Taylor, and the most popular girls at West Corner Middle School. Taylor never understood why they were so popular. They picked on all the other kids who weren't as rich and fashionably dressed as they were, which was almost everyone in the school.

As the Mansion Girls walked by Taylor still stooped to the floor, the fruity smell of expensive perfume trailed behind them.

Taylor's best friend Aleah, with bushy red hair that made her look like she had stuck her finger in an electrical socket and glasses too small for her face, rushed over to help Taylor.

Stephanie stopped in her tracks when Aleah darted in front of her. Stephanie flung up her hand like a traffic cop to halt Angela and Jennifer behind her. She then turned and spoke to Aleah. "Don't be in such a hurry, Fairy girl."

"Yeah, I bet you have a whole slew of Fairies living in that mop of a hairdo you have." Angela snickered.

"Is that Tinker Bell flying around your head?" Jennifer chimed in and the Mansion Girls cackled.

Taylor froze, unable to muster up the courage to defend her friend. The Mansion Girls might think she too believed in Fairies if she stood up for Aleah. Taylor didn't want to take the chance of getting ridiculed mercilessly like Aleah, who at the age of eleven still thought Fairies were real. Taylor desperately wanted to fit in and be popular. Disagreeing with the Mansion Girls, Taylor thought, was not the place to start. Stephanie walked on, but not without first purposely stomping Taylor's sandwich, crushing her bag of chips and then kicking her apple like a soccer ball. The apple rolled down the hall and was pulverized by the onslaught of 6th graders headed to lunch. The Mansion Girls laughed so loudly that Taylor was certain everyone in the whole school had heard it. Her face grew hot with embarrassment. As Taylor scraped her lunch up off the floor, she hoped one day they would get their just rewards, and she wanted to have a front row seat when it happened.

* * *

Later that afternoon, Taylor scrambled around in her kitchen while preparing the ingredients for a new chocolate recipe for tomorrow's "Chocolate and Gossip" competition. Taylor was still upset over the Mansion Girls ruining her last day of school. Baking and eating chocolate always made her feel better.

Taylor slid her glasses up close to her face and studied her freshly baked, chocolatey creation, then scattered one more hand full of rainbow colored sprinkles on top. She was sure this would be the chocolate recipe to finally win the contest and beat Sierra, who was both her friend and nemesis. Sierra had stick-straight mousey brown hair and a light sprinkling of freckles across her nose. Taylor jokingly referred to her in private as her "Fremesis". Not only did Sierra always win the Chocolate and Gossip contest, but what really got under Taylor's skin was that Sierra fraternized with her enemies, the Mansion Girls.

There were only three of them in the competition: her two best friends, Sierra and Aleah, and herself. So, Taylor had a pretty good chance of winning, even though she had never won. They met every Saturday and called their meetings "The Chocolate Gossip Party". They ate their chocolate creations, discussed the latest gossip and then voted on the best recipe and gossip story. Afterwards they posted it on their popular blog, "Chocolate & Gossip".

Now, when it came to making desserts, Taylor did not like following a recipe because she felt it limited her creative process. And Taylor often failed to read labels carefully, which usually resulted in a disaster; for example, there was the time she scooped from the salt bag instead of the sugar bag. If that wasn't bad enough, she used an old cake mix that had been in her kitchen cupboard far too long and had worms in it. Sierra had been the first to get sick that day and had accused Taylor of trying to poison them all.

"What the heck did you put in your recipe, Taylor? Are you trying to kill us? I think I'm gonna be sick!" Sierra had said accusingly.

"I don't exactly remember everything. I...um... changed

it up a bit." Taylor felt her stomach begin to tighten and gurgle.

"You need to learn how to read directions! And to use ingredients that aren't a hundred years old!" Sierra put her hand to her mouth and ran towards the bathroom.

It hit Aleah next. "Outta my way, Sierra!" She raced to the same bathroom, accidently knocking Sierra to the floor.

"No! I called it first!" Sierra got up and pushed Aleah back from the doorway and went in, slamming the door right in Aleah's face.

Aleah grabbed the only thing around, a potted plant in the hallway, and barfed into the dirt.

When Taylor's own stomach began to churn, she had no other choice, she opened her window and threw up all over her mama's beautiful blue Hydrangea.

That was the day the Chocolate Gossip Party girls ended up in the hospital. Taylor had felt horrible for making them all sick. Sierra had never let her forget it.

* * *

It was Saturday, the first day of summer break, and Taylor was excited about today's Chocolate Gossip Party meeting since it offered another chance to win the chocolate and gossip contest. Taylor thought she had a good chance of winning both today. Taylor pulled off the hair band she kept on her wrist - for times when her naturally curly hair got on her nerves, which was quite often - and tied back her dark brown hair. She placed her chocolate creation, which she ingeniously named "The Sprinkle Fest," in a container. Taylor felt her creations deserved a name in order to give everyone an idea of the tasty secrets that awaited them. For instance, she had named that disastrous recipe "The Chocolate Explosion", which had coincidentally ended up being just that.

Taylor headed out the door to Sierra's house, third house down on the right, with a note pad and "The Sprinkle Fest" in tow. No sooner had Taylor's feet hit the sidewalk when she saw them walking her way. Her stomach withered and gushed, like pouring salt on a slug. It was the Mansion Girls.

They were wearing their fancy riding attire, with the tight riding pants, high black boots and black velvet helmets. All the Mansion Girls had horses. Pangs of envy somersaulted in the pit of Taylor's stomach. She had always wanted a horse, but her family couldn't afford a horse, nor a mansion. Taylor didn't think it was fair that girls who were so mean could have so much.

As the Mansion Girls drew closer, Taylor pulled the band from her hair, letting it all fall in her face. She hid behind it like a curtain, hoping somehow the Mansion Girls wouldn't recognize her. Taylor didn't know why she even bothered, as they never noticed her anyway. But, if she won the chocolate contest….maybe then, Taylor thought, the Mansion Girls would notice her in a good way. They might even invite her over to go horseback riding like they did Sierra, after seeing her winning recipes on the "Chocolate and Gossip" blog. They always commented on Sierra's recipes, how scrumptious they looked and how creative she was. But if she won today, they could be saying that about her recipe.

When the Mansion Girls crossed to the other side of the road, Taylor let out a sigh. "Thank goodness," she whispered to herself. She watched as they sashayed across. Their long blond hair flowed down their backs like shiny sheets of yellow gold. Taylor imagined hearing the sounds "Rich…..rich….. rich" as their hair swayed from side to side in perfect rhythm.

What the heck were they doing in her part of the neighborhood, she pondered? Taylor had a hunch they were up to no good. Stephanie, Angela and Jennifer were headed right to the neighbor's house, the neighbor whom Taylor had just heard the creepiest gossip about.

2

Chocolate, Gossip and Lies, Oh My

Taylor knocked on Sierra's front door. She had a doozy of a gossip story to tell the girls and couldn't wait to see the looks of shock on their faces. It was a story she'd overheard secondhand from her mother, who had heard it firsthand, from their neighbor, Mrs. Beasley. Mrs. Beasley was known to be a great fabricator of gossip stories, so you never knew how much of it was true.

The girls were always trying to outdo each other with the chocolate recipes and the gossip, especially Taylor and Sierra. Taylor felt confident she would be the winner in both categories this time. It would be a first for her in either.

The door opened and Sierra stood there, grinning like a Cheshire cat. Her bangs were uneven as usual, because she liked to cut her own hair. A maroon and gold scarf was draped around her neck, which was odd, because Sierra never wore any kind of accessories.

"Hey Taytoe, let's see what you brought." Sierra bent down trying to peer into the sides of the container. "I hope you didn't use anything old in your recipe this time?"

"No, Sierra, I didn't. Do you have to bring that up every single time? Geez." Taylor rolled her eyes and walked right past Sierra.

"Well, it doesn't hurt to ask, just to be on the safe side. None of us like to vomit, ya know?" Sierra snickered.

Taylor ignored Sierra's comment and continued down the hall towards the kitchen, where Aleah waited anxiously. Masking tape was wrapped around the broken nose bridge of Aleah's glasses. She had painted it black with nail polish so no one would notice. However, everyone noticed and said it looked like a wad of black chewing gum stuck to the middle of her glasses. Strapped around her neck was a professional looking camera.

Aleah had been nominated official photographer for their blog. Taylor was under the assumption that Aleah thought she had been chosen because of her great picture taking abilities. But, truth be known, she was the only one who owned a camera. Aleah had once confided to Taylor, she fancied herself a great photographer, and had hopes of traveling the world, taking pictures of delicious food recipes for blogs and magazines. But for now, unfortunately, her pictures were always slightly blurred and a little off center.

"Where's the recipe card? You did bring one, didn't you?" Sierra asked Taylor as she followed her to the kitchen.

"No, I …..um…..didn't. But, I can look it up when I get home. It's my turn to do the blog this week, so I'll write it then." Taylor placed her dessert down on the counter for its proper photo shoot.

Taylor had not brought a recipe card because in her creative process of tweaking the recipe, she'd forgotten to write down all the changes. If she needed to, she could always improvise. She was good at improvising.

Aleah took pictures of Taylor's dessert, doing her best to look like a professional photographer, she bent down close, and then edged back, as to get every angle to make the dessert look tasty and delicious for the blog.

Taylor pointed over to the other recipes. "Now, who made which one?" Taylor asked, even though she could figure it out. Aleah's recipes were typically boring and by the book, but always delicious. Sierra was notorious for going over the top, by adding some sort of fancy candy decoration. However, there was the time she went overboard and lit sparklers on the top. It ended up catching Aleah's mom's paper tablecloth on fire. Taylor, in a panic, had thrown a pitcher of water onto the fire and unfortunately all over Sierra's dessert. The dessert was ruined. Sierra was devastated and accused Taylor of doing it on purpose. That was the only time Taylor came in as high as second place.

The girls headed to Sierra's room so they could begin discussing the new gossip.

Taylor stared at the scarf around Sierra's neck and adjusted her glasses. The huge lenses accentuated Taylor's big green eyes. Sierra had once told Taylor, "Green is an awful color for eyes. Brown eyes like mine are the best. They match anything you want to wear." Taylor knew that was only a jealous remark, but couldn't help herself and questioned the "matchability" of her clothes to her eyes ever since.

"Where'd you get the scarf, Sierra?" Taylor sat down on the rug and crossed her legs. Taylor couldn't imagine why Sierra would wear a heavy scarf in the heat of summer.

"Jennifer gave it to me; she told me she already had one like it." Sierra stroked the scarf like it was a coveted grand prize she had won at the State Fair.

"Oh, one of the Mansion Girls," Taylor said sarcastically. "Pffff!"

The Mansion Girls always wore expensive designer clothes; everything matched from their hair clasps to their toe rings. So, even a hand-me-down from them was nothing to throw rocks at.

"Don't be jelly, Taytoe. You can borrow it sometime, if you like." Sierra said, flipping one end of the scarf over her shoulder, then sat down on the rug across from Taylor.

Taylor shook her head "No thank you." Because it had once belonged to a Mansion Girl, Taylor would never admit she liked it. "I don't want a scraggly piece of wool wrapped around my neck, making me look like a Hogwarts Gryffindor reject."

"It's cashmere," Sierra said rubbing it up against her face. "It's soft, here feel." Sierra leaned over towards Taylor.

Taylor backed away as if Sierra was shoving a snake at her. "I'm not touching that thing; it probably still has Mansion Girl cooties all over it." Taylor patted the floor beside her for Aleah to sit down and join them. "Now let's get on with the meeting."

Taylor was anxious to tell her gossip story, but would have to wait for Sierra and Aleah to go before her.

"Ok, I go first since we are at my house today." Sierra's devilish grin didn't go unnoticed by Taylor. But she didn't care, for Taylor was certain her gossip story was going to top all.

"Ok, listen up, girls." Sierra said and lowered her voice, as Taylor and Aleah scooted in closer. "I overheard this last night at my mom's bunko party…"

"What's Bunko?" Aleah whispered to Taylor. Sierra's eyes widened and rolled.

"It's a stupid game where they roll some dice. Now, can I continue?"

"My dad says it's an excuse for the ladies to get together so they can sip wine and gossip," Taylor answered.

"Oh, sort of like us, only we eat chocolate and gossip….. and don't play with dice." Aleah looked over to Taylor for agreement.

Taylor nodded her head, "Right," then looked back to Sierra, "Ok, continue."

"One good thing about those Bunko parties, I get to hear a lot of juicy gossip. Listen to this. They found Mrs. Schmidt, the old German lady who lives three houses down from you, Taytoe, sittin' straight up in her arm chair, dead."

"Shut the front door! Dead?" Aleah shouted.

"As a doornail! Still holding her cup of tea in one hand and a wiener schnitzel in the other." Sierra's eyes were as big as saucers, looking back and forth between Taylor and Aleah, loving their response.

Taylor couldn't believe what she was hearing. The shock that Sierra saw on Taylor's face was not that of a person hearing some shocking gossip for the first time, but rather one of disbelief that ….Sierra was telling her gossip story! Hers!! The best gossip story ever told, in the history of the Chocolate Gossip Party. You couldn't make this stuff up. Her chances of winning….ruined!

"A wiener schnitzel with tea?" Taylor blurted out. "That's not what I heard at all! It was a crumpet. A crumpet you fool!

Ya know, tea and crumpets! Not tea and wiener schnitzel."
Taylor was furious, Sierra had stolen her gossip story, and
she could hardly think straight. The heat rushed to her cheeks
as the chance of winning the best gossip story flew out the
window.

"Tea and crumpets is more a British thing, not German.
Wiener schnitzel would stand to reason. Not sure about the
tea and schnitzel together though."Aleah didn't get to finish
before Taylor interrupted.

"You think because she's German, she can't eat a bloody
crumpet? That's the stupidest reasoning I've ever heard,
Aleah. Shut your pie hole." Taylor was furious at Sierra and
taking it out on poor Aleah.

Aleah sat motionless, mouth slightly ajar.

"Sorry, Aleah, I didn't mean to snap." Taylor half smiled.

"It's ok." Aleah smiled back.

"Does it matter what she was holding in her hand, a
crumpet, a wiener schnitzel, or a crumpety-wiener schnitzel?"
Sierra said, shaking her head.

"Yes, it does matter. We want to get the facts right for the
blog." Taylor snapped back.

"Ok, whatever. But it was a wiener schnitzel, so ya best
be writing that down in your little notepad. Now, if you don't
mind, I'd like to continue my story?"

"All right all ready." Taylor said, as she jotted down

"crumpet" on her note pad.

As Sierra continued the story of how they carted Mrs. Schmidt off in an ambulance, Taylor tuned her out. She pretended to jot down notes, but was instead, drawing tiny angry faces all over the page. Taylor was steaming mad at Sierra. Not only does Sierra almost always win the chocolate recipe contest, but now she had told the most awesome gossip story ever. A story Taylor felt was rightfully hers, after all, Sierra had never even met Mrs. Schmidt, and she had.

Taylor had to think quickly. Coming up with a story that would outdo Sierra's "Death of a Neighbor" story was going to be difficult, very difficult indeed.

When Sierra finished, Aleah went next. Aleah's stories were always long, drawn out and typically boring. So, while Aleah was going on with her story, Taylor feverishly pondered for her own story.

Taylor jotted down a word here and there from Aleah's gossip story, eyebrows knitted together as she racked her brain for an idea. This wouldn't be the first time Taylor made up some gossip to outdo Sierra.

There was the time Taylor told the outlandish fib about two of the Mansion Girls, Stephanie and Angela.

"Hey, I overheard some girls in the school bathroom today," Taylor had lied. "Angela found out Stephanie was sending secret love notes to Angela's boyfriend at school. So, to get even, she poured out Stephanie's expensive designer shampoo and replaced it with hair removal lotion. All her hair fell out, so now Stephanie has to wear a wig until her hair grows back."

The next day at school, Sierra snuck up behind Stephanie and yanked her hair hard. Stephanie screamed in pain, as it was no wig, but her real hair and Sierra ran. Which only proved Taylor's story was hogwash. Sierra gloated for weeks.

"Did you get all that, Tay?" Aleah leaned over to look at Taylor's note pad.

"Yes, I did." Taylor read out loud from her notes. "In short, Johnny T broke up with Jennifer because he saw her feet one day and noticed her second toe was longer than her big toe. It grossed him out and so he broke up with her. End of story. Did I miss anything?"

Johnny T was captain of the 8th grade football team and Jennifer, being a Mansion Girl, never had a hair out of place. So, for them to break up over what Johnny T thought to be an imperfection was big gossipy news.

"Nope, that's it in a nutshell. Remember to change the names to protect the innocent, and the guilty. The guilty being us." Aleah snickered. "We certainly don't want the Mansion Girls to hate us more than they already do."

Aleah and Sierra turned to Taylor and said in unison, "Your turn."

Beads of perspiration popped out on Taylor's forehead. She couldn't think clearly with them glaring at her, like a monkey in a cage. Think, think, think....she thought.

Then, Taylor recalled the day she and her mom had visited Mrs. Schmidt when she was sick. Taylor had been staring out Mrs. Schmidt's living room window when suddenly large winged insects swarmed from the bushes just below the window sill. Mrs. Schmidt had winked at Taylor, and told her they were Fairies. Taylor knew Mrs. Schmidt had been joking, but now it gave her the best idea ever.

As the rain began to fall, rhythmically tapping against the window, Taylor began to weave her story. This would be her best one yet, she thought.

3

Taylor's Big Fib

"A few weeks ago, I went with my mom over to visit Mrs. Schmidt. She hadn't been feeling well so we took her some soup and banana nut bread. We were sitting around her kitchen table and Mrs. Schmidt talked about her life story, how she was adopted at my age, 11, and grew up in Germany. She told how her family had to hide in a basement during the war and ate nothing but potatoes. Could you imagine that? Not even any chocolate."

"Get to the point, Taytoe. You're rambling," Sierra said, sounding annoyed.

There were times when Taylor didn't like it when Sierra called her "Taytoe," it was all in the way she said it. "When Mrs. Schmidt talked about her late husband, I got bored. So, I excused myself and went to the kitchen sink to wash my hands. I stared out the window waiting for the water to get warm, and that's when I saw it".

"Oh, no! Don't tell me you saw a ghost or a monster!" Sierra interrupted and bellowed out a forced laugh.

Aleah put a finger up to her lips in a motion for Sierra to be quiet.

Taylor continued. "There was a smoky white mist that hovered over what looked like a circle of stones. I couldn't really tell because of all the mist, ya know. I'd been standing there for quite a while before Mrs. Schmidt asked me if I saw it."

"Saw what?" Sierra asked, now curious.

"The Fairy Ring."

"Whoa, a real Fairy Ring?" Aleah asked.

"Yes, an honest to God Fairy ring, Aleah. I wouldn't make this stuff up." Taylor smiled nervously and adjusted her glasses.

"I did my summer project on Fairy Rings last year. I know quite a bit about them, but I've never actually seen one," Aleah said as she leaned in closer to Taylor. "Was the ring formed by mushrooms or stones?"

"How can you see anything, much less a Fairy Ring, from Mrs. Schmidt's kitchen window, when you've never even been in her house, Taytoe? You're making that up!" Sierra stood up and placed her hands on her hips. "You can't beat me on this one, Taytoe, so, don't even try."

But Taylor had been in Mrs. Schmidt's house. Taylor

recalled the first time she met Mrs. Schmidt. She and her mother stood in the foyer of the old Tudor house and she remembered how it smelled of old books, apple cider, and freshly baked bread. She liked it. She also liked Mrs. Schmidt, who wore her gray hair pulled up in a loose bun, and round, silver-rimmed glasses hung on the tip of her nose. A well-worn, but clean, white apron covered the front of her floral print button-up dress. Mrs. Schmidt was the very vision of what Taylor thought a grandmother should look like.

Taylor had lost the only grandmother she had known and loved when she was five. A favorite memory was on her fifth Birthday, her grandmother had given Taylor a pair of matching Hello Kitty lanterns. She loved those lanterns and missed her grandma to this day.

Taylor stood up and narrowed her eyes at Sierra, "I was in her house and I did see a Fairy Ring in her back yard! If you don't believe me go look for yourself!"

Taylor's heart shifted into high gear; she couldn't believe the words that spewed from her mouth. "Go look for yourself," Really? What was she thinking? She hadn't seen a Fairy Ring in Mrs. Schmidt's backyard that day, but it never occurred to her she'd have to prove it. She'd really backed herself into a corner this time. Taylor repositioned her glasses on her face and wiped the sweat beads that had collected on her forehead. She would have to come up with another lie when Sierra found out there was no Fairy Ring in Mrs. Schmidt's backyard, front yard or side yard. No Fairy Ring at all. Taylor wasn't sure if Fairy Rings could even exist in her neighborhood. She had never seen one or heard tell of anyone seeing one.

A quote from a poem that she'd been told many times by her mom, when Taylor made up stories, popped into her head.

"Oh what a tangled web we weave when at first we practice to deceive."

Aleah stood up, pressing down her shorts to try and remove the wrinkles that had formed while sitting, and joined Taylor and Sierra.

"How long ago was this, Tay? Fairy Rings don't last too long, if they're formed by mushrooms. I've always wanted to see a real Fairy Ring. This is incredibly awesome!" Aleah gave up on removing the wrinkles from her shorts. "Let's go now and check it out."

Taylor felt like plastering tape all over Aleah's mouth for even suggesting such a thing. She needed more time to think what to do. She felt a drop of perspiration trickle down the side of her face.

"Great idea, Aleah! Best idea you've had all day...no wait....make that all year!" Sierra laughed mockingly.

"Don't get mad at me because Taylor beat you in Gossip."

Aleah snapped back.

"She hasn't beaten me until she proves it." Sierra bobbed her head back and forth at Aleah. "Now, let's go check out that Fairy Ring."

Taylor began to panic, drops of sweat rolling down her face, as she pictured the three of them standing in Mrs. Schmidt's backyard, with nothing but overgrown grass, and Sierra pointing at her and laughing hysterically like those Mansion Girls had done that day in the school hall.

"Well, it might be gone by now. Like Aleah said, they don't last forever."

"I figured as much. There never was a Fairy Ring, was there, Taytoe?"

"Yes, there was, I mean is. Come on, let's go." Taylor was mad at Sierra for not believing her, even though Taylor's history for making up stories in the past would give Sierra a perfectly good reason not to believe her. And, of course, there was the fact that Taylor *had* made it up.

Sierra was the first to put her rain coat on. She found an oversized umbrella, big enough so all three girls could stay reasonably dry underneath it. Sierra opened the front door and was greeted by rain pouring down in sheets. Aleah was right behind her, standing on her tiptoes peeping over Sierra's shoulders.

Taylor stood in the hallway, fidgeting with a teardrop

earring hanging from her ear. It was one of a pair of earrings her Mother had given her six months ago for her 11th birthday. It was sterling silver and smooth to the touch as she rubbed it between her fingers to soothe herself. She didn't know how she was going to get out of this one.

Aleah turned around. "Come on, Tay. What are you waiting on? Fairy Rings don't last forever, ya know."

"Especially ones that don't exist," Sierra said, still looking out at the rain.

"Aren't you excited, Tay? Where's your raincoat?" Aleah asked Taylor, who stood like a statue in the hall.

"She would be excited, if there actually was a Fairy Ring to see, right...Taytoe?" Sierra sneered as she opened the huge umbrella and stepped out on the front porch.

Taylor let go of her earring, "I didn't bring a raincoat. And I am not that excited because I've seen it before, remember?"

Sierra rolled her eyes as she stood under the umbrella while the rain pounded down, dripping heavily off the sides. "Come on, guys!"

Both Taylor and Aleah stood with Sierra, huddled close under the umbrella, as the rain began to pour even harder.

"Okay, if we walk slowly and stay together we shouldn't get too wet." Sierra squinted trying to judge the distance to Mrs. Schmidt's house. Heavy rain made visibility practically impossible.

They stepped awkwardly off the front porch and walked slowly forward. Thunder began to rumble loudly off in the distance. The girls exchanged glances.

"It'll be alright, if we hurry before it gets any closer," Sierra said. Taylor thought Sierra was determined to waste no time in proving her wrong, and rationalized that getting struck by lightning might not be so bad after all.

"No it won't, Sierra. As bad as I want to see a Fairy Ring, it's not worth getting struck by lightning." Aleah cocked her head at Sierra and added, "Not for me anyway."

"Well I'm still going," Sierra huffed. "Taytoe, are you with me?"

Lightning struck so close that there was no time between the strike and the thunder; the girls' hair stood on end. All three screamed in unison, then turned and ran back to the house. Sierra stood on the front porch fiddling with the umbrella, trying to close it, when lightning struck again. Sierra ran through the door, with the open umbrella, flipping it inside out as it got caught on the door frame, exposing the metal framing underneath. Taylor was the last to come in, slamming the door behind her. All three stood in the foyer, the water dripping off them forming puddles on the floor. They looked at each other, then to the broken, inside-out umbrella, with its wire frame bent every which way but right and burst into laughter.

"I don't know why we're laughing, because we could've been killed," Aleah said, still laughing.

Sierra struggled with trying to fix the umbrella, water slinging up on the walls and in Sierra's face. She finally gave up and stuffed it in the hall closet that was so full when she shut the door, part of the umbrella poked out.

"Ok, no Fairy Ring today, but when it clears up let's plan a trip over to Mrs. Schmidt's back yard," Sierra said as she pushed up against the closet door making sure the umbrella wouldn't come bursting out.

"Sounds good to me," Taylor said as she looked back and forth between Sierra and Aleah. "Now, let's go eat some chocolate!" Taylor had never been so relieved in all her life.

The girls laughed and squealed as they raced down the hall to the kitchen to begin the chocolate feast.

4

THE Unexpected

The next morning Taylor awoke to the sounds of rain beating against her bedroom window. It was the sound of relief, knowing she still had time to figure out what she was going to do about the Fairy Ring. The crushing disappointment still lingered as she had come in last place, again, in the chocolate recipe contest. During her creative process, she forgot to add eggs, and the dessert turned out chewy and hard to swallow. She still held out hope for winning the best gossip, if she could create a believable Fairy Ring.

Taylor fumbled to find her glasses on the night stand, and slid them up to her face with one finger. She slipped on her Hello Kitty slippers and shuffled over to the window. Taylor pressed a cheek against the coolness of the window pane, and gazed over towards Mrs. Schmidt's house. How in the world could she conjure up a Fairy Ring that would pass Sierra's harsh criticism and Aleah's expertise?

Stones, she thought. Aleah had mentioned Fairy Rings could be formed out of stones. There might be enough stones in Mrs. Schmidt's backyard to form a ring.

Taylor got dressed, put on her galoshes, grabbed her favorite purple raincoat with a drawstring hood, and headed out the door. By the time she got to Mrs. Schmidt's house, the rain was barely a drizzle and the sun peeped from behind the clouds.

Taylor stood in front of Mrs. Schmidt's 2-story house, with its decorative and ornate dark wood trim that outlined the beige stucco facade. Taylor's mom said it was a Tudor house, a common style you would see in England or Germany. Colorful flowers of deep salmon, blue and yellow filled the window boxes that hung from each front window. With long, flowing greenery cascading from each, they were the most beautiful arrangements Taylor had ever seen. She was surprised she hadn't noticed them before now.

As she stood there, admiring the beauty of it all, she felt a sadness that she had not gotten to know more about the German lady who had lived here.

To the right side of the house, a small pathway led to the back, full of wet hanging overgrown branches. Taylor looked over both shoulders before sneaking around to the back yard. All she could do at this point was hope and pray there were enough stones to put together a Fairy Ring.

The backyard was open with an array of colorful flowers bordering the grassy middle that was on the verge of needing a trim. There in the middle of Mrs. Schmidt's backyard stood a single, large, white mushroom. One was not enough, but, at least it was a start.

Taylor panned Mrs. Schmidt's backyard looking for any halfway decent stones she could use to make a Fairy Ring. She looked behind and underneath bushes and plants, even digging dirt with her bare hands when she thought she spotted something. There was nothing. Nothing at all.

Taylor felt her heart sink like a wounded ship. Her lip quivered, tears filled her eyes but did not spill. She had no backup plan. Soon Sierra and Aleah would be at her front door ready to check out the Fairy Ring......a Fairy Ring that didn't exist.

The rain stopped. Taylor pushed her hood back and wiped her face, leaving streaks of dirt from her hands. She didn't care. Maybe she deserved dirt on her face, she thought, for getting herself into this predicament. Now she had to face the music of Sierra's ridicule and Aleah's disappointment.

As she turned to leave, a face peered out from the kitchen window. It looked like Mrs. Schmidt. But that was impossible. She was dead. Taylor's heart pounded in her chest.

The person disappeared and a moment later the backdoor

opened. There stood Mrs. Schmidt, in the same faded floral dress Taylor had last seen her in a week ago, with spectacles teetering on the tip of her nose.

"Get in here child and dry off before you catch your death of cold." Mrs. Schmidt motioned for Taylor to come inside.

Death....did she have to mention the word death, Taylor thought as she stood in shock, mouth opened, slightly shivering? How could this be? They must have been wrong about her death. All that crazy talk about dying with a crumpet or Wiener schnitzel, was apparently some gossip gone wild. Taylor rubbed her eyes, and pinched herself until it hurt. She was not dreaming. Mrs. Schmidt was still there.

"Missy, get in here and out of dat vet grass. Come have some hot cocoa and pastry to varm you up." Taylor loved Mrs. Schmidt's German accent.

Taylor's mouth watered at the mention of pastries. Rumblings in her stomach reminded Taylor that she had not eaten breakfast. She walked as slow as she dared, hoping Mrs. Schmidt wouldn't notice her apprehension. What if it was a trap, and she was being lured in by delicious pastries? After all, this woman was supposed to be dead. What else might be wrong, she wondered? Poison pastries? Fattening her up for the oven? The lyrics from a song popped in her head as she walked towards Mrs. Schmidt.

"*Will you walk into my parlor, said the spider to the fly.*"

Mrs. Schmidt helped Taylor with her raincoat and hung it on a carved wooden coat rack that stood tall in one corner. The top reminded Taylor of deer antlers and she wondered why anyone would want to cover it with coats and hats. The kitchen was bright and cheerful with painted green cabinets. It was the cleanest kitchen she'd ever seen, everything was neat and in its place. The smells of baked apples and sweet pastries permeated the room. Taylor's stomach growled loudly.

"Have a seat, Sweetie and I vill get you dat hot cocoa." Mrs. Schmidt turned to get fresh cream from the refrigerator, when Taylor interrupted her.

"And the pastry.....you did say pastry didn't you, Mrs. Schmidt?" Taylor scooted her chair in closer to the table and she licked her lips, thinking about fruit-and-cream-filled pastries. Taylor glanced over to Mrs. Schmidt's oven and thought it was much too small for her to fit inside.

"Yes, I did. You hungry dear?"

"Yes, Mrs. Schmidt, starving actually," Taylor hesitated, "You are Mrs. Schmidt, right?" Taylor asked and did her best to pull back her lips into a smile that didn't look nervous.

"Of course, Dearie, who else vould I be?"

"I was....um.... making sure you didn't have a twin or something." Taylor said, with a half-smile. "And it's Taylor."

Mrs. Schmidt poured cream in a pot on the stove. Taylor

watched a small flame light from underneath. Mrs. Schmidt retrieved a mug from the cabinet that looked even older than she was, turned to Taylor and smiled.

"What's dat, Sweetie?"

"Taylor.....my name is Taylor. Taylor May Dawson, three houses down. I brought you some soup and banana brea...

"I know who you are love, and I know your name. I just may never call you by your name. Vill dat bodder you, Sweetie?" Mrs. Schmidt placed the mug of steaming hot cocoa in front of Taylor along with a plate of freshly baked pastries with bits of apple filling oozing from the seams.

Taylor didn't mind at all. In fact, she loved it. It warmed her insides and she felt safe and comfortable in the kitchen with Mrs. Schmidt. "Doesn't bother me at all. I love being called sweetie and dearie and stuff. I never liked my name that much anyhow." Taylor grinned.

"You eat up and sip dat hot cocoa nice and slow. It's quite hot." Mrs. Schmidt began to clean up what was already an immaculately clean kitchen, while Taylor sipped her hot cocoa and scarfed down two whole pastries. They didn't taste poisonous at all, she thought. They were perfectly fine, but she might need one more, to be sure.

Mrs. Schmidt pulled up a chair and sat down across from Taylor and stirred her hot cocoa. "Vhat's a sweet little girl like you doing digging around in someone's back garden?"

"Oh, that....well." Taylor looked down and fidgeted with her napkin still folded neatly by her plate. "I-I was looking for stones, Mrs. Schmidt. I had no idea you'd be home. I thought you were dea... um... not here. I'm sorry, I should have asked." Taylor did her best to avoid the truth, without telling a fib. It felt wrong to lie to Mrs. Schmidt, unlike lying to her friends which was perfectly alright in times of desperation.

"Not to vorry. But you should always stand on da side of caution vhen venturing into unknown places." Mrs. Schmidt smiled and peered over her spectacles.

"Oh, for sure." Taylor nodded and smiled back but had no idea what Mrs. Schmidt meant.

"So, tell me Sweetie, about your little get-togeders vith your friends."

Taylor's mouth dropped open and a piece of pastry fell out. "How do you know about the Chocolate Gossip Party?"

"Oh, Sweetie, is dat so important how I know? Besides, the neighborhood is not so big, people talk ya know."

"Yeah, they sure do, and it's not always right." Taylor decided not to mention to Mrs. Schmidt that she was supposed to be dead. Taylor picked up the piece of pastry that had fallen out of her mouth and popped it back in.

Taylor told Mrs. Schmidt all about the meetings, the blog, and most importantly, in her opinion, how Sierra was usually victorious in the chocolate contest.

"Vhy is it so important to vin dis contest? Is it not fun to be vith friends to talk and eat chocolate?"

"Yes, that part's fun. But ya see....well....there's these popular girls, who don't like me, but they post comments about how yummy Sierra's winning chocolate recipes are. And now, Sierra is friends with them."

"And you vant to be friends vith girls who don't like you?"

"Well, when you say it like that, it sounds crazy. But they have horses and Sierra gets to ride those horses."

"So, it's all about riding horses?"

"No, not exactly." Taylor fidgeted with her earring." I want to fit in and have it all together like the popular girls and not be such a dork that I can't even make a chocolate recipe people can eat without throwing up."

Mrs. Schmidt nodded, "Now, dat makes sense."

"Vould you like me to teach you a recipe that vould give Miss Sierra a run for her money? You might even vin. I have lots of delicious recipes."

Taylor was so excited to hear this; she nearly knocked over her mug. Taylor didn't understand what "a run for her money" meant, but she did understand, quite clearly, what "might even vin" meant.

"Oh, for sure!! That would be awesome! Thank you. Um..... Do you have some chocolate recipes? As long as it has chocolate in it or on it, I don't care which." Taylor wanted to hug Mrs. Schmidt, but remained seated because she felt it would be awkward.

"I most certainly do. You come over later dis afternoon and vee vill pick a recipe togeder. Ok....Yes?"

"That sounds good to me. I can come right after lunch, if that's ok?"

"Anytime is good for me." Mrs. Schmidt leaned in closer to Taylor. "Now, to get off dee subject a bit, I need to tell you someting very important about dat Fairy Ring."

Taylor stopped sipping her hot cocoa. "Um....w-w-what Fairy Ring would that be?" Taylor felt the heat rush to her cheeks, how could Mrs. Schmidt possibly know about her Fairy Ring, she wondered, that she made up?

"Da von you vere looking for in my back garden. You remember dat one....yes?" Mrs. Schmidt cocked an eye over her glasses and winked at Taylor.

Well, yeah, Taylor thought. How could she forget?

"Oooooh...that Fairy Ring," Taylor said trying to sound like she had genuinely forgotten about it and shifted nervously in her seat.

"Yes, Mrs. Schmidt, I know about that one, and that there's not one. I wanted to beat Sierra at the contest, since she stole my gossip story." Taylor confessed, then realized that Sierra's gossip story didn't hold true anymore either, because Mrs. Schmidt was apparently alive and well.

"I thought I could make a Fairy Ring using stones from your backyard, but you don't have Jack squat. Believe me, I checked." Taylor pointed to the dried dirt smeared on her face.

"I may be able to help you out vith dat as well."

"Really? That would be great."

"But vith all decisions come consequences. Some good, some bad."

"Sure, yeah. Consequences. How soon can you help me? Because, I'm gonna need one pretty soon." Taylor, at this point, didn't care about consequences. Besides, what could possibly go wrong with a Fairy Ring.......a Fairy Ring that wasn't even a real one?

"You come vith me."

Taylor followed Mrs. Schmidt to the kitchen window.

"You look over dare."

Taylor looked to where Mrs. Schmidt pointed. Over to one side, piled up under a mulberry bush, was a stack of smooth, white stones. How in the world had she missed those? They couldn't have been there before, she thought.

"Are you pointing to those stones?"

"Yes Dearie, I tink dey vould make an excellent Fairy Ring. Vhat do you tink?

"Yes, I think they would. But I swear I didn't see them before."

"Sometimes vee get in such a hurry, vee cannot see for looking." Mrs. Schmidt tapped Taylor's mug. "Now, let's go finish our cocoa."

Oh, dear Lord, there she goes again saying things that made no sense, and besides, Taylor thought, she had looked and didn't see them. Taylor was almost positive that they weren't there before.

Mrs. Schmidt placed another pastry on Taylor's plate. She reached over and placed a hand on Taylor's, before Taylor could take a bite. "Now listen carefully. Dat big mushroom vill be the starting point of da Fairy Ring. You must den draw an "x" on da ground vith your finger before you place each stone. You understand?"

"Sure, but why's that?"

"You don't vant to go open up a portal to da Fairy World, Sweetie." Mrs. Schmidt smiled and winked at Taylor.

Taylor was glad she winked, because for a moment, she thought she was serious.

"A nudder ting, you keep an eye on your friend Sierra, she is one to be watched around dat Fairy Ring. Even a made-up Fairy Ring can still possess some magical properties, if it has at least von mushroom connecting da ring. So, you keep her straight." Mrs. Schmidt peered over the top of her glasses. "You can do dis? Yes?"

Taylor gently slid her hand away, not only was Mrs.

Schmidt's hands icy cold, but it made her uncomfortable Mrs. Schmidt, knew anything about Sierra, much less what she'd do around a Fairy Ring. "Well.....sure, Mrs. Schmidt, I'll do my best."

"And dat's all you can do." Mrs. Schmidt wrapped up the last of the pastries in parchment paper and handed them to Taylor.

"Da best ting for you to do is go learn as much as you can about Fairy Rings before you show it to your friends."

Mrs. Schmidt helped Taylor with her raincoat.

"Von more ting."

"Yes, Mrs. Schmidt?"

"Tell no von you came here or dat vee talked. We don't vant everybody coming over here to learn about Fairy Rings and chocolate recipes. It vill be our secret, ok Sweetie?"

"Ok, Mrs. Schmidt," said Taylor resignedly. That ruined her plan for letting Sierra know she, as well as the whole neighborhood, was wrong about Mrs. Schmidt being dead. "Thanks for the pastries."

"I vill see you dis afternoon and vee vill bake and talk. Ok, Liebchen?"

"Ok, Mrs. Schmidt. I'm looking forward to it." Taylor had no idea what a Liebchen was, but didn't want to waste any more time by asking; she had a Fairy Ring to make.

Taylor placed all the stones in a circle, using the mushroom as the starting point, and made a Fairy Ring anyone would be proud of, well, except for Sierra.

On the way home, Taylor was disappointed she couldn't tell Sierra that she had been wrong about Mrs. Schmidt. However, she was elated that she would have a Fairy Ring to win the gossip contest. A thought occurred to her, had she drawn an "x" under every stone? She couldn't be sure. Not that it mattered, she was sure Mrs. Schmidt was pulling her leg about opening a portal.

5

FaiRY Rings

Taylor hid the wrapped pastries inside her raincoat before going inside. She ignored her mom calling out to her and hurried upstairs to her room. She was quick enough to hide the pastries underneath her pillow before her mom walked in.

"Did you not hear me call you, young lady?"

"Yes, Mama, I was in a hurry to get to my room to get off my wet raincoat, before I catch my death of cold." Taylor smiled hoping to ease her mother's anger.

"That's no excuse. From now on, you answer me when I call you. Understood?"

"Yes, Mama, I'm sorry."

"You need to get downstairs and take out the trash in the kitchen, like I asked you to do yesterday." Her mom glanced around her room and frowned like she smelled something foul. "Then, clean up this pig sty of a room. I can't even see your floor with so much junk on it. It looks like a tornado came through here."

"Ok, ok, Mom, I vill." Taylor snickered. "I mean I will."

As her mother turned to leave, Taylor asked, "Hey, Mama?"

"Yes?"

"Did you go to Mrs. Schmidt's funeral?"

"Yes, honey, about the whole neighborhood went. Good thing we did; she had absolutely no family there. Kinda sad really, you know?"

"Did you actually see her in the coffin?"

"Heavens no. She was cremated and put in a lovely red urn. Red of all colors, I would have thought gold or silver, but not red, maybe it's some sort of German tradition. Who knows?"

"So, you never actually saw her dead?"

"Good gracious no, Taylor. You don't go peeping in an urn at a funeral to make sure they're in there. How crazy would that look?"

"Yeah, I hadn't thought about that."

As soon as her mama left, Taylor plopped on the bed and stared at the piles of clothes and stuff scattered across her floor and her mind began to wander. How could Mrs. Schmidt be in an urn somewhere, cremated, when she just saw her? Taylor didn't think a ghost could bake and make hot cocoa. But why would she fake her own funeral? It didn't make sense. "There's a needle in that haystack you don't want to find, because it may prick you," her dad would say. And Taylor didn't want to go looking for that needle, because she didn't want to know the answer. She needed Mrs. Schmidt's help with a winning recipe and she didn't think she could stay in her kitchen long enough to learn it, if she knew Mrs. Schmidt was a ghost.

After taking out the trash and cleaning up her room, she was surprised how much stuff she managed to shove under her bed, and keep hidden by the bed skirt. She would deal with it later, later being whenever her mom discovered it. Right now, the most important thing was to find out more about Fairy Rings.

Taylor sat on her bed and leaned back on her comfy pillows with her laptop. She reached under the pillow and pulled out the pastries. She researched Fairy Rings and munched on deliciousness. She found lots of interesting information; this included how they emerged after a rain, the different types of mushrooms, and how long they usually last, which was only about a week. However, they could re-emerge after another rain. Some were made of stones and permanent. Blah, blah, blah.... this was mostly boring stuff, which did not help her at all. Until, finally, she came across a website about the magic and mysteriousness of Fairy Rings. Ok, here we go.

Fairy rings have a long history in European folklore, with different cultures believing they represent different things. Usually they symbolize a place where elves, pixies, or fairies appear to dance and play. As fun as that sounds, most cultures viewed them as dangerous places for mere humans. Better to avoid them, then to get caught up in magic you don't understand.

Those who know the fairies will tell you that fairy rings are where the Fairies dance and perform many of the rituals of their own magic. Legends warn you that those who join the Fairy dance within the circle under the moon are sometimes lost to time and place. They may even disappear from mundane space forever.

Taylor read on and on about Fairy Rings and their magic, mysteries and origins. Although she found it intriguing, she wasn't sure why she needed to know any of this. Was there something Mrs. Schmidt had wanted her to know? Taylor hadn't believed in Fairies since she was six when she found out Tinker Bell wasn't real. But now, after reading about Fairy Rings, she was beginning to believe that strange things could happen in and around a Fairy Ring.

She sat there, twirling her hair, wondering what Mrs. Schmidt meant by keeping Sierra straight around the Fairy Ring. Maybe she'd heard about Sierra burning Aleah's mom's tablecloth, and didn't want her backyard on fire. Taylor couldn't remember if she told Mrs. Schmidt she would keep Sierra straight or not. Who could do that, Taylor thought?

Certainly, not herself, if Sierra didn't know how to behave around a Fairy Ring, then whatever happened would be Sierra's fault.

The quote popped in her head, loud and clear, only this time it was in the German voice of Mrs. Schmidt.

"Oh vhat a tangled veb vee veave, vhen first vee practice to deceive."

Taylor certainly had no intentions of purposely deceiving Mrs. Schmidt. All she knew was that Sierra was responsible for her own behavior.

More times than not, Taylor hated to read, but she did find reading about Fairy Rings quite entertaining. Taylor finished off both pastries, wadded up the parchment paper, and stuffed it under her bed.

Taylor walked over to her window, pulled back the curtain and saw Sierra and Aleah strolling up her driveway laughing and talking. She imagined Sierra was telling Aleah how funny it was going to be when they went to Mrs. Schmidt's backyard and found there was no Fairy Ring. She watched as Sierra threw back her head and cackled. And she imagined Aleah trying to convince Sierra that Fairies were real. Taylor could hardly wait to show them her Fairy Ring. Aleah would be so excited and Sierra would be devastated.

Taylor slipped on her clogs and headed downstairs, when the doorbell rang.

"I'll get it." Taylor hollered out to anyone in ear shot. Taylor's little brother, Jordan, was usually preoccupied with his favorite action figure or watching a kiddie show on TV. He wasn't allowed to answer the door by himself anyway. Taylor's mom was in the kitchen; she could hear her shuffling around with the sounds of pots clanging.

Taylor opened the door to an excited Aleah, who had an ear to ear grin spread across her entire face and was bouncing up and down on the balls of her feet. Sierra was wearing her familiar smirk.

"You ready to go check out that Fairy Ring Taytoe?" Sierra covered her mouth with her hand, pretending to mask the snicker.

"I sure am." Taylor ran back to the kitchen to tell her mom that they were going for a walk and would be back soon.

Jordan came sliding out of his bedroom in his sock feet. "Hey Sierra, Blue Guy got a scrape on his knee." Jordan held up his favorite action figure for Sierra to see.

"Hey hey hey Jordy! Let me look." Sierra examined Blue Guy, kissed the knee and handed him back to Jordan. "Here ya go, Jordy. He's as good as new." Sierra ruffled Jordan's hair.

"Thanks!" Jordan grinned and raced back to his room.

"I don't know why he likes you so much, Sierra," Taylor said, shaking her head.

"He's so cute and sweet, I don't know how you two can even be related, Taytoe." Sierra said and wobbled her head at Taylor.

"Oh, would you two stop and let's go!" Aleah said, while opening the front door.

As they walked out the door, Jordan came back out of his room with mismatched clothes on and cowboy boots. "I want to go see the Fairy Ring too."

"Shhhhhh…..Jordy. You've got to stay here. I'll take you another time, ok?" Taylor said in a hushed voice.

"No! I want to go now or I'm telling Mama!"

"Oh, let him go Tay. What's it gonna hurt?" Aleah grabbed Jordan's hand.

"All right Jordy, but don't you dare tell Mama about the Fairy Ring. She'd ground me for life." Taylor informed her mama she was taking Jordan with them on their walk.

They headed down the sidewalk towards Mrs. Schmidt's house. Taylor noticed Sierra was carrying a camera. "What's the camera for, Sierra?"

"I want to take a picture of your face, when we find out there's no Fairy Ring. I'd like to post it on the blog, along with a picture of some weeds and dirt. With a caption in big bold letters, "Taylor's imaginary Fairy Ring." Ya know, another one for the records. Like that disastrous chocolate recipe that made us all sick. You remember that don't ya,

Taytoe?" Sierra laughed so hard she snorted.

"How can I forget, Sierra, when you constantly remind me? I'm surprised you didn't take a picture of us throwing up and post that to the blog." Moments like this were when Taylor questioned why she was even friends with Sierra.

"I would have...." Sierra was laughing so hard she could hardly get the words out. "...If I hadn't been throwing up myself."

"I can't wait to see it, Tay," Aleah said.

"See what, a picture of my face on the blog?" Taylor frowned at Aleah. Sierra's relentless picking and jabbing was getting to Taylor, and once again, she snapped at Aleah.

"Simma down, Tay. I was talking about the Fairy Ring." Aleah reached over and placed her hand on Taylor's shoulder and whispered, "Don't let her get to you. Not worth it."

"Sorry, Aleah." Taylor twisted up a half smile at Aleah.

"I want to remind everyone about the rule for not stepping inside the ring. That goes for you too, Jordy. That would be bad business, very bad." Aleah said and grabbed Taylor's arm to slow her, so Sierra could go on ahead.

Sierra didn't even notice they had fallen behind as she was in such a hurry to get to Mrs. Schmidt's backyard.

Aleah leaned into Taylor and whispered. "Sierra asked to borrow my camera, I figured so she could take pictures of the Fairy Ring. I'm sorry for that."

"Don't worry about it, Aleah. She'll get what's coming to her. Besides, there is a Fairy Ring."

"I thought so, Tay. I always believed you. I knew you wouldn't make something like that up."

Taylor shrugged her shoulders and shook her head, "Why would I?"

Sierra turned around and hollered, "Come on, Jordy and Fairy Ring girls! Get the lead out and come on!"

They ran and caught up with Sierra.

6

Bad Luck

It wasn't long before they stood in front of Mrs. Schmidt's house. The grass was high from the recent rain. The flowers hanging from the window boxes were dead. Taylor wondered how they could've browned and withered so quickly since this morning.

"Ok, girls, follow me." Taylor held onto Jordan's hand and led them through the hanging wet branches towards the backyard. Sierra was directly behind Taylor, so a couple of times Taylor accidently let a wet branch sling back in Sierra's face.

"Hey! Watch it with the wet limbs, Taytoe!! They're going right in my face!"

Taylor turned around, trying not to laugh or even smile, when she saw Sierra's wet face, "Oh, sorry, Sierra. I didn't realize you were so close behind me." Taylor hadn't done it on purpose, but, Taylor thought, that's what Sierra gets for being in such a hurry to prove her wrong.

"Be more careful. I'm getting soaked back here." Sierra wiped her wet face and slung water back on Aleah.

"Hey, Sierra, knock it off!" Aleah accidently stepped on the back of Sierra's heel, making her shoe come off, and Sierra stepped right into a mud puddle.

"Oh great, just freaking great! I'm with a couple of fools looking for a nonexistent Fairy Ring, I'm getting soaked by flying wet branches, and now my foot is caked with mud!" Sierra stopped and bent over to get her shoe back on her foot.

Taylor kept walking and mumbled under her breath "We'll see who the fool is."

"Wait for us, Tay!" Aleah hollered out and watched Sierra scrape mud off her foot with a stick and fumble to get her shoe back on. "You need some help, Sierra?"

"No thanks to you, I've got it. And don't you dare walk past me. I want to be the first one there to get that picture of Taytoe's face. Now, back up."

"Actually, you would be the third one."

"What?" Sierra's expression was one of annoyance and confusion.

"Tay would be first, next Jordy, then yo…."

"Can ya shut your pie-hole, Aleah?" Sierra looked back at Aleah whilst struggling with getting her shoe back on her muddy foot.

While Sierra was bent over fumbling with her shoe, Aleah

had later confessed to Taylor that she had the urge to reach over with her foot and push Sierra down, face first, right into the mud puddle. Naturally, Aleah, being who she was, did not. But Taylor and Aleah had giggled at the thought of it.

"Come on, slow poke girls!" Taylor hollered as she waited at the entrance to Mrs. Schmidt's backyard.

"I wouldn't be a slow poke if it weren't for you two," Sierra said as she caught up to Taylor, with Aleah right behind her.

Taylor stopped abruptly when she stepped into the backyard, causing Sierra to run right into the back of her with Aleah following suit by running into Sierra. Taylor's heart jumped to her throat and began to choke her. Her stomach knotted and she could hardly breathe. The Fairy Ring was not there. Not even the mushroom.

"Ok, where is it?" Sierra said, turning her head back and forth as if she were watching a tennis match.

Aleah whispered softly in Taylor's ear, "It is here, right, Tay?"

Taylor's hands felt wet and clammy. She thought she was going to hurl the pastries she'd eaten earlier.

They crept closer into the back yard and there, amongst the overgrown grass, the Fairy Ring appeared to emerge like a mirage in a desert.

"Look girls, there it is." The relief of seeing the Fairy Ring, allowed Taylor to breathe again, and she was quite proud of her masterpiece. Taylor looked over at Sierra, whose jaw had dropped nearly to the ground. She was standing, stunned, with her wet freckled face and one mud-caked foot.

They stood there for a minute staring at the Fairy Ring. A smile grew on Taylor's face that you couldn't wash off, as she basked in the glory of seeing the astonished look on Sierra's face.

"Sierra, hand me the camera, I want to take a picture of your face" Taylor reached over, acting as if she were going to take the camera from Sierra. "I'm going to post it to the blog, with a caption in big bold letters. "Here is Sierra's face when she finds out Fairy Rings are real."

Sierra quickly snapped out of her bewilderment and snatched the camera out of Taylor's reach. "Oh, stop it! It's just a bunch of rocks, that's all it is!"

"I'm pretty sure that's a real Fairy Ring. This one is special, though; it has rocks and mushrooms….well, a mushroom." Aleah did her best to smile without smirking at Sierra.

"Yeah Sierra, a bunch of rocks that happens to be in a circle, called a Fairy Ring." Taylor waved her arm over towards the Fairy Ring as if she were a game show host presenting a prize.

Aleah took her camera back from Sierra's slightly limp hand. "Since you won't need this now, Sierra, I want to take pictures of my first real Fairy Ring."

Sierra, begrudgingly let Aleah take back her own camera. "This is crazy! A bunch of rocks in a circle doesn't make it a Fairy Ring. You could have made this, Taytoe. You're still gonna have to prove it by me. I'm not gullible gulenstien like Aleah here."

"Gullible what?" Aleah frowned and then snapped a picture of Sierra's angry face.

"Oh, come on, Sierra, how much more proof do you need?" Taylor leaned over and lightly touched the top of the large mushroom.

"Actually, it can be proven. But it would be dangerous, and we are not doing that." Aleah went back to snapping pictures of the Fairy Ring.

"How?" Sierra walked over and stopped right at the edge of the Fairy Ring and kicked the air above the large mushroom. "This is silliness."

Aleah looked at Sierra like she had lobsters crawling out of her ears. "Be careful, Sierra. You can't go stepping inside a Fairy Ring without following the proper rules. And you certainly don't want to destroy it by kicking a mushroom." Aleah grabbed Sierra's arm and gently pulled her back away from the Fairy Ring's edge.

"What do you mean by how, Sierra? How can it be proven or how's it dangerous?" Taylor asked.

"Both." Sierra shook Aleah's hand off her arm and

stepped right back up to the edge of the Fairy Ring. "I am not afraid of a stupid mushroom Aleah, nor this thing you call a Fairy Ring."

"Well, did you forget what I told you guys the other day about stepping inside a Fairy Ring?" Aleah asked as she snapped another picture.

"Refresh my memory, Aleah." Sierra huffed and rolled her eyes. "I wasn't really paying attention to you that day, because I don't believe in Fairy Rings, or Fairies, or Elves or anything like that. Besides, you know how you like to ramble on, so I tuned you out."

"Well you better listen up this time, because if you're not careful, you could get in big trouble." Aleah was more than serious, but Sierra only laughed.

"Right, right. So let's hear it........ again" Sierra huffed and rolled her eyes, which she'd become proficient at doing, especially when it came to hearing things she thought were a complete waste of time.

Taylor listened while Aleah repeated to Sierra the proper way to step inside a Fairy Ring, and about the bad luck that would befall them if they didn't do it right. Taylor wasn't concerned about it, after all, this Fairy Ring wasn't even a real one. Taylor glanced over to the kitchen window. It was as dark as night inside. It was hard to believe that just yesterday it was bright, cheerful and filled with the smells of fresh baked pastries, steaming hot cocoa and the presence of the, seemingly, not-so-dead Mrs. Schmidt.

"So, you're telling me, if I come back at midnight, on a full moon and run around the Fairy Ring nine times, counter clockwise, I will be able to step in the Fairy Ring properly and see some real Fairies?" Sierra asked, as she tapped the top of the mushroom with her foot.

"Yes, Sierra, I said possibly see some Fairies. Stepping inside a Fairy Ring without doing all that, you could be stuck with bad luck the rest of your life, or it's possible that you could disappear...... forever. You must show respect around a Fairy Ring, and that means not walking through one or stepping in one. Or worse, destroying one."

"Yeah right, that's hilarious, Aleah."

"Now would you stop tapping that mushroom with your foot. You are asking for trouble, I tell ya." Aleah tried to grab Sierra's arm again, but Sierra was too fast and jerked away. Sierra lost her footing, tripped over Aleah's foot, and fell right into the Fairy Ring.

Taylor watched Sierra as she wallowed around in the wet grass trying to get up. The seat of Sierra's pants was soaked and smudged with grass stains and dirt. She couldn't help but snicker. In the back of her mind she could hear Mrs. Schmidt's voice. "Sierra is one to be watched around a Fairy Ring." Well, that was certainly true. She was quite entertaining right now.

"Oh, my gosh, Sierra! Quickly, grab my hand!" Aleah leaned over, being careful not to cross over into the ring with her foot, and stretched out her arm to Sierra.

"Shoo, Aleah! I don't need your help! I am totally drenched now! And it's your fault!! Look at me, I'm a mess!" Sierra got up, brushed herself off as best she could. She walked out of the Fairy Ring, but not before purposely stepping right on the large mushroom, toppling it off its stem.

"Sierra, what are you doing? Are you crazy??" Aleah stood there, paralyzed from shock.

"Why'd ya wanna go and do that for, Sierra? You got no home training, ya know that?!" Taylor didn't think any Fairies would be angered by Sierra destroying their property, but it was the only part of her Fairy Ring that was real.

"Fairy Ring, Smairy ring, I've seen no proof." Sierra walked over and kicked the mushroom like it was a football trying to make a field goal. The mushroom broke into a million pieces as it flew across the air and scattered all over Mrs. Schmidt's backyard.

Taylor's stomach clinched at the sight of this and she looked over at Aleah in horror. She knew Aleah would be mortified. In all her innocence, bless her heart, Aleah still believed in Fairies and their magic, be it good or bad. And according to Aleah, this was bad for Sierra.....very bad.

Aleah ran over and began picking up the pieces of the pulverized mushroom, mumbling under her breath, "What have you done Sierra?"

Jordan stood in shock, mouth wide open, and grabbed his sister's hand. He'd never seen Sierra act like this.

"It's useless, Aleah. You can't pick up all those pieces." Taylor felt sorry for Aleah and mad at her at the same time. She wanted to shake some sense into her and tell her to wake up and smell the bacon, there was no such thing as real Fairies. But Taylor figured Aleah was not ready for the truth, even at age 11. Maybe next year she would break it to her gently, but for now, Aleah needed a friend to believe in her. Poor thing got picked on something fierce by other girls at school about it, especially the Mansion Girls.

"Not by myself I can't. You all get over here and help me." Tears trickled down Aleah's face. She didn't even look up as she combed through the grass, picking up pieces of white sponge.

Sierra looked over at Taylor and said under her breath, "She's a little sensitive today, isn't she?"

"Not really." Taylor lowered her voice. "Give her a break Sierra. We need to back her on this. Besides, I don't know why she's upset; it's you that the Fairies would be angry with, not Aleah nor me."

"Come on you guys." Sierra glanced over at Aleah and

back to Taylor. "No harm done, it's a stupid mushroom." Sierra walked over and squatted down by Aleah, picked up a tiny piece of mushroom, held it up in front of Aleah's face. "See, it's harmless. Not worth crying over. Not one tear."

"You don't understand, Sierra. When you desecrate a Fairy Ring it brings you bad luck. Not for a day, but the rest of your life! Just because you don't believe, doesn't mean it won't happen." Aleah continued picking through the grass.

Sierra placed the mushroom piece on top of the crumbled pile cupped in Aleah's hand. "Aleah, you're hopeless," Sierra said.

"Come on Aleah, even if you picked up every piece of mushroom, there's no way we could put it back together. What's the point?" Taylor said.

"This will definitely make the Fairies angry. This is not good.....not good at all." Aleah sniffled and used her shirt tail to wipe the tears from her face.

"Ok think for a minute, Aleah, you know a lot about Fairy Rings, maybe there's something Sierra could do to fix it. Surely there's something you learned from that Fairy Ring project that's useful," Taylor said hoping she didn't sound condescending.

"I can't fix that mushroom, Taylor, surely you jest." Sierra darted her eyes over at Aleah. "And I can't fix stupid either."

"Not the mushroom, you idiot. I'm talking about what

you did." Taylor shook her head.

"Well, there is one thing she could do." Aleah stood up, carefully holding the pieces of mushroom in her hands. She walked over and gently placed them in a pile from where they had once stood whole.

"What's that, Aleah?" Sierra asked, and with a quick jerk looked over to Taylor. "And by the way, Taytoe, I'm not an idiot."

"Well, you're sure acting like one." Taylor snapped.

"Well, you would know." Sierra snapped back.

"Um..um." Aleah cleared her throat. "Can I have your attention please?"

Taylor and Sierra stopped arguing, and listened to Aleah.

"Midnight, full moon, remember how it goes, Sierra?" Aleah asked.

"No way am I coming here at midnight by myself."

"You wouldn't be alone, Tay and I would come with you."

"Not me, Aleah. You can come with Sierra, but my parents would never let me come here at midnight."

"My mom wouldn't either, Aleah. That's crazy." Sierra said.

"That's why we can't tell them, we'll have to sneak out. We need to come up with a plan soon, because there's actually a full moon tonight." Aleah said.

"Are you sure it's tonight?" Taylor questioned.

"Another summer project, Aleah?" Sierra asked.

"Yes, Tay, it's tonight. And no, Sierra, I find the moon interesting." Aleah forced a smile.

"Who in the heck does projects over the summer anyway? Summer is for having fun, swimming, eating ice cream, having sleepovers, staying up all night and getting into a little trouble," Sierra said, shaking her head at Aleah. She turned to Taylor and said out of the side of her mouth, "What a weirdo."

Taylor widened her eyes at Sierra in hopes that she would not make fun of Aleah. Sierra had a habit of talking about people within ear shot, thinking they couldn't hear her, but they always could.

"Well, summer's just started Sierra and you've already gotten yourself into some trouble." Aleah said.

"Trouble with who, Fairies?" Sierra laughed.

"Maybe, but you definitely got yourself some bad luck coming your way." Aleah responded.

Taylor glanced over at Aleah and smiled. That's when she saw Jordan throwing the stones from the Fairy Ring into the bushes.

"Jordy! Stop that!!" Taylor ran over and grabbed a stone from his hand. "What are you doing?!"

"If there's no Fairy Ring, Sierra won't be in trouble."

"That's not how it works Jordy. We gotta put the stones back." Aleah reached down to grab a stone. "Come on girls, help me."

Taylor whispered to Aleah, "Ya know, he meant well."

"I know, Tay. But I'm sorry to say, he's in for a heap of bad luck too."

"That can't really be true, Aleah. It's probably superstition." How could it be true, when the Fairy Ring was fake, Taylor thought, but she couldn't tell them that.

"We've got to come back before midnight. Sierra and Jordy will need to bring some sort of a peace offering to place in the middle of the Fairy Ring. After the ninth run around, you jump inside the ring and place your peace offering, maybe say you're sorry or something, and step out as quickly as possible. You don't want to linger inside a Fairy Ring. That should break the bad luck spell."

"Sorry, Aleah, but Jordy and I will not be coming here tonight. That's not gonna happen. My parents would kill me, especially if I drug Jordy along with me."

"You should seriously consider it, Tay, if you want to remove the curse from Jordy. Sierra, looks like it's you and me."

"Not gonna happen, Aleah, it would be too creepy. A person recently died here. There are probably remnants of her spirit still lingering here. No freakin' way."

They finished putting the stones back in place and turned to leave. Standing there, blocking the pathway, were the lovely Mansion Girls.

"What we got here?" Stephanie said as she led the Mansion Girls into the backyard.

"Did I hear something about a Fairy Ring?" Jennifer asked as she examined the rock formation.

"Yes, that's right. A real Fairy Ring." Aleah answered.

"Oh look.....it's the Fairy girl." Angela said condescendingly.

"It's only rocks in the grass, we're out here messing around. Besides, we were just leaving," Sierra sounded nervous and forced a smile.

"I don't know why you hang out with these losers, Sierra." Stephanie said and looked over at Taylor and Aleah. "It doesn't look good for you."

Jennifer and Angela stepped in the Fairy Ring and spotted the broken mushroom.

"Look at this, Jennifer." Angela spread out the piled-up pieces of mushroom with her Gucci pointed-toe shoe.

"What is that?" Jennifer said, as she smashed it with her foot.

"Stop that! It's a mushroom and you shouldn't be stepping on it like that," Aleah said, cringing as they continued to mash it into the ground.

"Why not? Will your Fairy friends come after us, Fairy girl?" Angela said sarcastically and walked over to Aleah.

"Probably," Aleah whispered under her breath.

Angela stood right in front of Aleah, "What did you say, Tinker Bell?" Angela was close enough for Aleah to smell her croissant and strawberry jam breath.

Taylor stepped forward, draped her arm around Aleah's shoulders, and spoke to Angela. "The Fairies may not get you, but there's a ghost in that house that loves designer clothes and fancy stuff, so, if I were you, I don't think I'd hang around here too long." Taylor pointed to Angela's stylish shoes. "If you wait a minute, you can see a ghost at that back window."

All three Mansion Girls turned at once and stared for a moment at the kitchen window.

"We certainly don't scare easily, Recipe Disaster Girl, but we have riding lessons to attend, so we were leaving anyway," Stephanie said to Taylor, then turned to Sierra, "We look forward to your next delicious recipe on the blog Sierra." The Mansion Girls spun on their designer shoes and left.

They stood without speaking, until the Mansion Girls were out of sight. Then all four solemnly walked out of the backyard, Aleah leading the way with Jordan and Taylor bringing up the rear.

As they walked through the hanging branches, by the side

of the house, a loud snap came from above. Taylor looked up in time to see a large limb falling.

"Look out, Jordy!" Taylor pulled Jordan out of the way, within inches of being hit.

"Girls, if that's not a sign, I don't know what is, I didn't think it would start so quickly." Aleah said and looked up to check for the threat of more falling limbs.

"A sign of what?" Taylor said as she helped Jordan step over the limb.

"Bad luck," Aleah sighed.

"It's a coincidence." Sierra said trying to sound confident, but instead, it came out sounding like a squeaky toy.

"Let's get out of here before any more limbs decide to fall." Taylor turned around one last time, glancing back at the house. She thought she caught a glimpse of Mrs. Schmidt's face peering out the kitchen window, but at second glance there was only the reflection of a cloud passing in the sky.

On the way back to the house, a large flock of black birds flew over, squawking and chirping loudly. Taylor and the rest looked upwards to the ruckus in the sky. Bird droppings fell like heavy rain drops, splattering on Sierra and Jordan like paint balls.

"Come on, let's run!" Sierra shouted, using her arms and hands to protect herself from the bombs of bird poop.

They ran and screamed, "The birds, the birds!" Jordan

stumped his toe, tripped and fell on the sidewalk. All the girls stopped and helped Jordan up and saw that both of his knees were scrapped badly and bleeding. Jordan began to wail.

"Everything will be alright, Jordy," Taylor said and inspected his wounds. "Let's get you back to the house and get you a bandage." Jordan loved bandages, especially ones with his favorite characters on them. Once he had snuck the box of Power Ranger Band-Aids from the cabinet and put every single one on his arms and legs.

"You have to dry up your tears, Jordy, and you can't tell Mama, she'd kill me for letting this happen to you."

Jordan did his best to not cry, but it was hard. He was scared and bleeding. "Is that my bone sticking through?" Jordan sniffled.

"No Jordy, it's only your skin. You're gonna be fine. Now let's go get you fixed up." Taylor glanced over at Aleah and Sierra. "What the heck's going on here?"

"I'm telling you, Tay, it's the bad luck spell, curse, or whatever it's called, but I'm here to tell ya, it's only going to get worse." Aleah said under her breath, so Jordan wouldn't hear. "You should come with me and Sierra tonight."

"I never said I was going, Aleah. How thick is your skull?" Sierra said sarcastically.

Taylor looked down at Jordan, and the pangs of guilt gripped her insides. This could all be a bunch of foolishness, because the Fairy Ring wasn't even real. But what if it wasn't foolishness, she thought, what if their believing made the curse real? She'd heard about the power of suggestion, but this was ridiculous. She cringed at the thought of how much worse the bad luck could get. And it would all be her fault.

"Alright, I'll go. But this sure better work, Aleah, because if I get caught tonight, my life is over."

"That means you too, Sierra." Aleah cocked her eye at Sierra.

"All right already! But I'm only doing it for Jordy, not for you two fools." Sierra grabbed Jordan's other hand and they all headed into Taylor's house.

7

THE Plan

When they arrived back at Taylor's house, the mud on Sierra's foot was dried and cracked. Taylor led Sierra around to the side of the house and hosed down her foot.

"Mama would make me clean the whole house if you tracked mud inside. To be on the safe side, let's leave our shoes on the porch."

After they removed their shoes, Aleah insisted they be lined up in color order, from light to dark, and arranged them accordingly. Sierra was busy wiping her foot on the welcome mat trying to remove any remaining signs of mud.

They were hot, sweaty, and mentally exhausted. Taylor opened the front door; the air-conditioned air hit them in the face like a splash of cold water. It was refreshing. Sierra wiped her foot one last time on the inside mat, as she did not want Taylor's mom mad with her for tracking in mud. Mrs. Dawson liked Sierra and she did not want to blow that.

Aleah's mom, on the other hand, did not care for Sierra ever since the burning of the table cloth incident.

"Mom, we're baaack!" Taylor hollered out to her mom, who was still in the kitchen, then whispered to Jordan. "Go upstairs to my bathroom and I'll bandage your knees. Whenever Mama sees your bandages, tell her you fell in the backyard."

"Okie dokie," Jordan said, and hobbled up the stairs.

"You girls, want something to eat?" Mrs. Dawson asked from the kitchen.

Taylor looked over at the other girls and they all nodded enthusiastically.

"I could eat a cow right now," Sierra whispered under her breath, "dipped in chocolate," and licked her lips.

"I certainly couldn't eat a cow, Sierra, but I'm so hungry my stomach is caving in." Aleah clutched her stomach.

"Ewe....that's gross, Sierra." Taylor said.

"Well, I'm so hungry......even gross would taste good right now." Sierra made a mooing sound and laughed. The girls giggled.

"Yes, Mom, we would love some food! We'll be up in my room!" Taylor shouted back to her mom. "Come on girls.... let's go." Taylor raced up the stairs, two steps at a time to her room, with Sierra and Aleah hurrying close behind her. One might have thought a herd of buffalo was trampling up the stairs.

After getting Jordan bandaged up, Taylor joined Sierra and Aleah in her room. Taylor reached in the top drawer of her bedside table, pulled out a mechanical pencil and a dog-eared blue composition book, with a big Hello Kitty sticker smack dab in the middle.

"Ok girls, let's get this plan figured out." Taylor plopped down on the circular white shag rug, reached back and pulled her hair up into a ponytail. "Come on girls, sit down." Taylor opened her composition book, ready to take notes. "Ok Aleah, tell us what we need to do to get rid of this stupid bad luck thing."

"Well, ok, first of all….."

Sierra abruptly interrupted Aleah, "Hello Kitty? Really, Taylor, how long have you had that notebook, since you were like 5 or something?"

"News flash, Sierra….. Hello Kitty is for all ages, dummy."

"Girls, please! I don't think either one of you are grasping the seriousness of the situation. Now can I continue?" Aleah said, and appeared to be totally frustrated.

"Sorry, Aleah, go on." Taylor raised an irritated eyebrow at Sierra.

"It would help if I had the book 'Fairy Rings and Pretty Things Aren't Always Good', but I had to turn it back into the Library last week. Oh well, I think I can remember enough to help us get rid of the curse."

"You think? Don't you need to know for sure?" Taylor questioned. "This is my little brother were talking about."

"And me!" Sierra snapped.

"Ok, Sierra your peace offering has to be something of value to you, not money value, but like....emotional value. Tay, you'll have to get something of Jordy's too."

"Like something sentimental?" Taylor asked.

"Yeah exactly" Aleah responded.

"You got something like that Sierra?" Taylor wondered if Sierra had sentimental feelings for anything other than that scarf around her neck.

"I sure do."

"Bring it tonight." Aleah said.

Anger brewed insider Taylor. She thought that if it hadn't been for Sierra stealing her gossip story, she never would've made up the Fairy Ring story. And Jordy wouldn't have the bad luck curse and she wouldn't have to go to Mrs. Schmidt's backyard at midnight and dance like an idiot in the moonlight. Even though, technically, she wouldn't be the one dancing or running around the ring. It didn't matter, Taylor thought, they were all going to look stupid tonight. And it was all Sierra's fault.

The bad luck that had happened to Sierra and Jordan today seemed very real. But had it all been a coincidence, she wondered, or had she created a Fairy Ring that was more real than she intended. Taylor didn't want to take any chances, and felt she had no other choice but to do what it took to fix it.

"So, is that it? The peace offering will break the bad luck thing?" Sierra said impatiently.

"Well, I think so."

"What do you mean....you think so?" Sierra said as she stood.

"Well, it's all hypothetical. I've never done this before," Aleah answered.

"Hypo.....shmypo, it better work." Sierra smarted off, then walked to the window.

"What if Sierra brings a piece of junk. Something she doesn't really care about?" Taylor asked Aleah in a hushed voice, keeping her eyes on Sierra. "Do you really think it will matter? Maybe the curse isn't real."

"Don't dare try to trick the Fairies. You saw the bad luck that's already happened to Sierra and Jordy. That's real, Tay," Aleah said loud enough that Sierra heard.

"Oh, why not?" Sierra laughed. "I think they should be happy we're giving them anything at all!"

"You're playing with fire if you do, Sierra. You may anger them to the point of no return."

"What does that mean, Aleah?" Taylor asked.

"Well, they might take her in."

Sierra jerked her head around to Aleah, "Take me in where?"

"Their world."

"Yeah, right." Sierra shook her head and gazed out the window. "Hey you guys, come take a look at this, hurry."

Aleah and Taylor jumped up, raced over to the window in time to see a swarm of tiny bodied insect like creatures with exceptionally large wings flying out from the bushes below.

"What in the world are they?" Taylor had her whole face pressed up against the window.

"Are they even insects?" Sierra lightly nudged Taylor out of the way as to get a better look.

"What else would they be?"

"Maybe they're Fairies?" Aleah wedged herself in between Taylor and Sierra.

Sierra grabbed Aleah's shoulders, spun her around to face her and lightly shook her back and forth. "What kind of world are you living in, girlfriend?"

"One where anything's possible.....like Fairies flying by a window. Now let me go." Aleah shook Sierra's hands off her shoulders and turned back to watch as the large-winged, insect-like creatures flew out of sight.

"Let's have a sleepover at my house. It's Friday, and that means wine night for my mom. She's out like a light by 10ish, so sneaking out won't be a problem." Sierra suggested.

"That would work for me, and Jordy would love that." Taylor glanced over to Aleah waiting for her response. How Aleah's mom felt about Sierra was no secret between the girls.

"I don't think I can do the sleepover." Aleah nervously scratched the back of her neck, she awkwardly looked down, avoiding Sierra's stare. "I can sneak out and meet you all over at Mrs. Schmidt's mailbox at 11:45 tonight. How does that sound to everyone?"

"That'll work," Sierra said, still eyeing Aleah.

Taylor thought Sierra felt more hurt than anger over Aleah not being allowed to spend the night. Taylor couldn't help herself and felt sorry for Sierra.

"Taylor, do you have a couple of big flashlights you can bring over? I don't think we have a flashlight."

"I have a nice big Hello Kitty lantern I'll let you borrow Sierra. You can pretend you're five years old and going out on a midnight adventure." Taylor did a side glance at Aleah and grinned. Aleah said nothing, but a huge smile spread across her face like a splitting seam.

"You got to be kidding me, right?"

"No, here I'll show you."

"Don't you have normal flashlight, for goodness sake?"

Taylor opened her closet door and reached up on the top shelf, pushing aside piled-up clothes and a box labeled "Old

Diaries". She pulled out a Hello Kitty, handle held lantern. "No, I don't, Sierra, this will work fine. Nobody's going to see you anyway. It's going to be midnight with nobody but us, the Fairies, and their ring.....oh wait.....are you worried about the Fairies making fun of you for carrying a Hello Kitty lantern?"

Sierra rolled her eyes and snatched the lantern from Taylor's hand, "Does this piece of junk even work?" Sierra turned on the switch and began to shake it wildly, hitting the side with her palm.

"Easy now, Sierra, I'm sure it needs new batteries." Taylor reached back in the closet, pulled out another lantern and quickly spun around grinning. "Lookie, Sierra, we'll be matchers." Taylor held up another Hello Kitty lantern.

"I swear you couldn't make this stuff up if you tried." Aleah chuckled and took the lantern from Sierra. "I really like these." Aleah held it up, turning it at all angles, admiring it.

"Well, at least I won't be the only idiot walking down the side walk, at midnight, with a huge freaking Hello Kitty light." Sierra grabbed the lantern back from Aleah and her admiring eyes.

The girls jumped from a sudden knock on the bedroom door. In walked Taylor's Mom carrying a tray of lemonade, sandwiches and chips. The girls thanked Mrs. Dawson as she left the room, and commenced eating like there was no tomorrow. Fairy Ring investigating had worked up an appetite in all of them.

Taylor knew she had to go back over to Mrs. Schmidt's house that afternoon, not only to tell Mrs. Schmidt everything that had happened, but most importantly, in her mind, to learn that chocolate recipe.

Taylor walked the girls to the front door and told Sierra, she and Jordy would come over later, before dark. As soon as they were out of sight, she flew out the door with her pencil and Hello Kitty notebook and headed back to Mrs. Schmidt's for another visit.

8

THE TEA PARTY

Taylor was breathing so hard her chest hurt when she knocked on Mrs. Schmidt's back door, for she had run the whole way. Taylor bounced anxiously up and down on the balls of her feet waiting for Mrs. Schmidt. The door opened with an overpowering smell of baked apples and cinnamon mixed with the aroma of fresh brewed tea. It was so intoxicating it made her sway and saliva rushed from underneath her tongue.

"Come in my Liebchen," Mrs. Schmidt said as she pulled Taylor in and put her arms around her. Mrs. Schmidt held her in so closely, it was like Taylor was being pressed into an apron-wrapped marshmallow.

Taylor really liked the old German lady, a lot. She especially liked the way she smelled, like a bakery shop with a hint of old book smell.

"I vasn't sure if you'd be back or not my sweets." Mrs.

Schmidt let go of Taylor and motioned for her to have a seat.

"You've got to teach me that recipe, Mrs. Schmidt. Besides, I love coming here. And I have some interesting stuff to tell you too." Taylor's eyes looked right past Mrs. Schmidt and feasted on the food set out on the kitchen table.

In the center of the table was a three-tiered silver dish. Oozing lemon-curd squares lightly dusted with powdered sugar filled the bottom. The second layer was crammed full of chocolate divinity balls. On the top dish, piled high, were thick, coconut sugar cookies with a glazed candied cherry stuck in each center. Next to that sat a large silver bowl filled with every color of fruit imaginable. Two china place-settings, patterned with dainty pink roses, sat neatly on the table. Drool dripped from Taylor's mouth and she wiped it with her sleeve.

"Oh, my goodness, Mrs. Schmidt, are you expecting company?"

"Yes, my Dearie, it's you." Mrs. Schmidt led Taylor over to the place set for her. "Have a seat Sweetie. Vould you like some tea?" Mrs. Schmidt reached over, grabbed the teapot and began to pour before Taylor could answer her. "I love a good tea party." After pouring the tea, Mrs. Schmidt plopped in two cubes of sugar, and poured fresh cream from a matching cream pitcher. "Now stir and tell me vhat you tink, Lovey."

Taylor had never had anything other than sugar in her tea, and if she were adventurous, maybe a slice of lemon. Slowly she put the cup to her nose and took a big sniff.

"Go on, Dearie, don't be afraid, it's not going to bite you."

"I've never had cream in my tea before." Taylor said, holding the rim close to her lips but still not sipping.

"Der's alvays a first time for everyting. If you don't like it, vee vill pour it out and start over......yes?"

Taylor nodded and sipped her tea. "It's good. I mean really good. I didn't think I would like it.....but I do." Taylor sipped again and again until it was gone.

Mrs. Schmidt placed another dish on the table. Stacked high in a pyramid were brownies that had a dollop of caramel coconut frosting. "Try von of dees." With silver tongs, she set one on Taylor's plate.

Taylor picked it up with her hand, forgetting all about the fancy silver utensils laid out for her to use, and took a huge bite. "Oh wow, Mrs. Schmidt, these are killer brownies......I think I died and went to heaven!" Taylor took another bite, then shoved the rest in her mouth and licked her fingers.

"Vould you like me to teach you dis brownie recipe for your contest?"

"Oh gosh yes! Sierra will be so jealous!" Taylor picked up her empty teacup. "May I have some more tea please?"

"Help yourself, Love, den you come over to da stove and

I vill show you how to make dis recipe. Afterwards, we can sit and have our tea party and vee can talk."

Taylor loved Mrs. Schmidt's heavy German accent. She could sit there all-day sipping tea with lots of cream and sugar, eating goodies and listening to her talk. Taylor finished off her second cup of tea, then slid her chair back, making a loud scraping noise against the wooden floor. With her Hello Kitty notebook and pencil in hand, she went and stood beside Mrs. Schmidt. All the ingredients needed to make the German Chocolate Brownies, were laid out on the counter.

Taylor wrote down every step along the way, in between the mixing and measuring. Mrs. Schmidt told Taylor she would remember it best if she did all the work herself. After the frosting was made, Mrs. Schmidt and Taylor sat at the table while the brownies baked.

"Vould you like another cup, Sweetie?" Mrs. Schmidt held up the tea pot.

"Yes please, I think one more." Taylor pushed her cup closer to the Tea pot and Mrs. Schmidt poured, leaving enough room for the cream and sugar. "Thank you."

"Get you some food, Sweetie."

Taylor grabbed one of each sweet, not caring if she looked greedy. She had never tasted food so good as Mrs. Schmidt's in all her life.

Taylor noticed Mrs. Schmidt's plate was empty. "You not

gonna eat, Mrs. Schmidt?"

"Someone has to test all dis food before you eat it, to make sure it's edible. And dat person is me.....I'm stuffed to da gills. But I vill have some tea whilst you tell me what you were so out of breath about at my doorstep. Did someting happen today? Someting about da Fairy Ring I imagine?" Mrs. Schmidt peered over the top of her glasses at Taylor and raised her right eyebrow.

Taylor swallowed down a big chunk of chocolate divinity and quickly took a big gulp of tea to finish washing it down. "I...uh....yeah. You were right about Sierra. She does not know how to behave around a Fairy Ring.

"Oh, vhy am I not surprised. So, you go on and tell me."

Taylor proceeded to tell Mrs. Schmidt of the day's events including the part about Jordan and all the bad luck that followed him and Sierra, but mostly him. Mrs. Schmidt poured herself another cup of tea and added a tad more to Taylor's cup.

Taylor wasn't getting the response of shock she expected from Mrs. Schmidt so she continued.

"I don't believe in Fairies, but the bad luck thing seems real. Is that even possible, since this Fairy Ring is not a real one? You think it's a coincidence? Jordy can be accident-prone at times. And Sierra, well she's a hot mess with everything.... except for winning chocolate contests."

"Yes, dat is very possible. But I tink vhat's more possible, is dat you may have created a real von. If you missed drawing even von "x" under a stone, den you vould've created a portal to da Fairy World. Den you have a Fairy Ring dat's not so fake anymore."

"I tried really hard, really I did. But, I could've forgotten one. Anyway, it doesn't matter, because I'm gonna fix it tonight. We're gonna get rid of the bad luck curse."

"Vhat about Sierra, how is she handling all dis?"

"Sierra doesn't even pretend to believe in any of this and is kicking, screaming and complaining the whole way. But she is going to come tonight."

"Vell, you do vhat you can to keep her in line. Don't let her anger get to you."

"She makes it really hard sometimes." Taylor looked away. "So hard sometimes, I don't want to help her."

"You vill figure it out, I have fate in you."

Taylor thought Mrs. Schmidt meant to say faith, not fate, but couldn't be sure with her German accent. Taylor was glad she told Mrs. Schmidt their plans, but an uneasiness still brewed in the pit of her stomach. Could she have created a real Fairy Ring? Was a portal to the Fairy World dangerous? Surely Mrs. Schmidt would have warned her. It was too much for her to think about. All she wanted to do was get rid of the bad luck for Jordy and Sierra and be done with all this nonsense.

Mrs. Schmidt pulled a box from a drawer in the buffet and handed it to Taylor.

"I vant you to have dis."

"What is it? Taylor opened the box. Inside was a necklace made with light brown colored beads.

"It is a necklace made from berries of a Chinaberry tree. My adopted mother made it for me, ven I vas about your age."

"It's beautiful, Mrs. Schmidt, but I can't accept something your mama made you."

"The first-time I vore it, I found out I vas allergic to da berries. My skin vould break out terribly. I could never vear it. So please, take it and vear it. Vear it for good luck.

"I love it, Mrs. Schmidt, thank you." Taylor put the necklace around her neck.

"You know, it is said dat if a Fairy touches a Chinaberry, dey vill pass out in an instant."

"Well, I don't think we have to worry about that." Taylor touched the beads and snickered. "Thanks so much for the Tea Party, Mrs. Schmidt, and for teaching me the German Chocolate Brownie recipe. I will let you know if I win next time." Taylor tucked her notebook under her arm and headed towards the door.

"Here, you take dis." Mrs. Schmidt had wrapped up some

goodies for Taylor to take with her. "Share vith Sierra if you like, maybe it vill sweeten her up a bit." Mrs. Schmidt winked and smiled at Taylor.

"We can only hope." Taylor smiled back.

"Von more ting, Sweetie. After you finish your little run around da Fairy Ring, you must remove each stone den place a circle from da spot you took it. Den stack dem back vhere you got dem. Dat vill close da portal if you've opened von."

"Ok sure."

Before leaving, Taylor turned and hugged Mrs. Schmidt. "Mrs. Schmidt, what is a Leebshun, that you call me sometimes?"

"Awe, my Sweets." Mrs. Schmidt cupped her hands around Taylor's face. Her hands felt cold to Taylor's flushed cheeks. "It's a German vord, means like sweetie or sweetheart."

"Oh ok. Well, I like that word." Taylor's heart warmed. "You gonna be home tonight? I hope we won't disturb you." Taylor envisioned Mrs. Schmidt peeping out from underneath the lid of a red urn, watching them run around the Fairy Ring.

"I vill alvays be here ven you need me." Mrs. Schmidt smiled and winked.

9

THE Midnight Fiasco

Taylor and Jordan arrived at Sierra's house later that afternoon, before the sun disappeared behind the trees. They came with their sleeping bags in tow, two Hello Kitty lanterns, and an old "Woody" doll that used to be Jordan's favorite toy for his peace offering. Stowed away in an overnight bag were Mrs. Schmidt's delicious homemade goodies.

Taylor insisted on Sierra showing her right away what her peace offering was going to be. Taylor knew Sierra was not one to share her feelings. Taylor had never seen her care much for material things, except for that stupid Gryffindor scarf Jennifer gave her. Taylor thought Sierra wouldn't take that off her neck long enough for it to be used as a peace offering, even if she got it back soon after. Taylor was curious to see what object Sierra would have any attachment to.

Sierra sat down on her soft bed and swung her legs over,

leaving no room for Taylor or Jordan. Taylor sat down on a hard wooden, squeaky chair with no arms. Jordan sat on the floor beside her and entertained himself with Blue Guy.

"So, let's see it Sierra. Where's your peace offering?" Taylor shifted, trying to get comfortable. It was the most uncomfortable chair she'd ever sat on in her life.

Sierra reached over and picked up a small wooden music box off her bed side table. She unlatched a small metal hook on the front and pushed back the wooden lid. A tiny ballerina with a pink tutu, white stockings, and a blond bun, popped up and slowly spun as the music played.

"I love this music. Listen to it, Taytoe, isn't it beautiful?" Sierra stood up with the music box and swayed and twirled, holding it out in front of her like a dance partner. It was as if she and the music box were the only ones in the room.

"Yes, I know that music. It's "Fur Elise" by Beethoven. My dad plays that all the time on the piano." Taylor didn't think Sierra had listened to a word she'd said. Taylor watched Sierra as she waltzed around the room with the music box.

Sierra finally stopped for a moment, still slightly swaying, as if she had come out of a drunken spin. "What was that, Taytoe?"

"The music......its "Fur Elise"......by Beethoven."

"I didn't ask for a card catalog description of the music, I asked if you liked it, dummy."

"Yes, I like it. My dad plays it all the time on the piano."

"I don't care if your dad plays tiddlywinks. I simply asked if you liked it....geez."

"Do you have to be so mean all the time Sierra?"

"As a matter of fact, Taytoe, I wasn't being mean. I was only speaking the truth. I can't help it if the truth hurts. Besides that, you need to quit rambling on with useless information when someone asks you a simple question."

Taylor's backside was going numb from sitting too long, so she got up and walked over to where she had plopped down the sleeping bags. She untied the ropes and rolled hers out on the floor, revealing a slightly worn pattern of white Hello Kitty faces all over the top side of a pink background. She sat down feeling frustrated with Sierra and her sassy attitude. "So is that your peace offering?..........The music box?.......... Sierra?.........Helloooo?"

Sierra ignored Taylor's questions and held the music box out in front of her, turning it this way and that. She smiled, admiring the dark brown wooden box shaped like a Pirates treasure chest, and watched as the pink ballerina disappeared when she closed the lid. Sierra glanced over at Taylor with a half-smile and a slight gleam in her eye, "My dad gave me this on my eighth birthday, the day before he left........." Sierra's smile flattened. "...... and never came back." The gleam in her eye vanished.

It had been three years since Sierra's family had moved into the neighborhood. Shortly thereafter, her dad left, never returned, disappeared without a trace. Sierra never talked about him until now.

"Ya know.....it's kinda funny." Taylor said as she quickly leaned over and searched for the goodies in her overnight bag. She was not comfortable with the sadness that seeped from Sierra's eyes. Taylor had never seen Sierra cry.

"What's funny?" Sierra asked and quickly wiped her face.

"That a pink tutu wearing, dancing ballerina would be put in a music box that looks like a pirate's chest." Taylor pulled out the package full of goodies. "Hey, look what I brought...." Taylor held up the delicious goodness wrapped up neatly in parchment paper. "Ya hungry?" Taylor was still slightly full of the earlier stuffing she did at Mrs. Schmidt's Tea party. But, she would rather be preoccupied with stuffing her face, than dealing with Sierra's emotions of sadness. Emotions, Taylor thought, Sierra didn't possess.

"I'm hungry! Can I have one too?" Jordy asked, while holding Blue Guy up in the air flying him around.

"Sure, Jordy." Taylor motioned for him to sit on her sleeping bag.

"What's so funny about that?" Sierra's face crunched up into an awful frown.

"Well, can you imagine a pirate and a ballerina together?

I think it's funny....that's all."

"Well, I have news for you, Miss Taytoe. Did you know that Bluebeard, the pirate, was in love with a ballerina for years?" Her name was...Anna Kerina ..... or something like that, and when she died from scurvy, which means she had a vitamin C deficiency, he buried her in a wooden box shaped like a treasure chest." Sierra's face twisted and knotted up even further. She placed a hand on her hip and wobbled her head from side to side. "I bet you didn't know that, did ya?"

"What's scur....scurrey?" Jordan asked.

"No, I didn't know that, along with a billion other people, because it's not true." Taylor wasn't sure if it were true or not, but she felt sure this was one of those wild stories Sierra made up, and threw in a fact or two, for example, the vitamin C and scurvy, to make her whole story appear true.

"You should try reading more books, Taytoe. It's in all the history books. I know.....because I've read them."

"Anna Karenina is a princess from a book. Not a ballerina."

"I said Ker-ina, not Kar-enina. Open your ears, Taytoe. And if she's from a book, I'm surprised you would even know about it, seeing as you don't read."

Taylor had not read the book. It was her mom's book, and a thick one at that. Taylor didn't like reading books, especially thick ones.

"Whatever, Sierra." Taylor didn't want to argue any further. "So, is that your peace offering or not?"

"No, don't be silly. That old music box means nothing to me. I love the music it plays, that's all." Sierra sat on her bed and placed the music box back in the same spot, very gently, as if she were placing the crown jewels back on its velvety stand. "But this......." Sierra opened the top drawer of her bedside table and pulled out a necklace.

Taylor got up and walked over to get a better look. She stood there, slightly confused, as she gazed at the necklace dangling back and forth like a pendulum from Sierra's hand. It was a cheap necklace one might get from a machine in a grocery store lobby. Hanging from a tainted silvery chain, with bits of fuzz and strings clinging to it, was a large blue stone glued on so haphazardly to the front of a silver ornate inlay that it was not properly centered. The chain was knotted up and kinked in places as if it had been tossed in the drawer without care. Taylor looked from the necklace to Sierra's face and back to the necklace. "*This* is your peace offering?"

"Yeah....what's wrong with that?" Sierra balled it up and stuck it in her shorts pocket.

"That necklace is something you love and cherish, and have an emotional attachment to?"

"Why would you doubt me, Taytoe? I have lots of emotional attachment to this necklace. My mom got it for me when I was......I think I was.....like nine or seven or something." Sierra did a kind of half shrug with one shoulder and looked away from Taylor, then continued with her story.

"I stayed home from school one day all sick with strep throat, which is short for Streptococcus, a bacterial infection, ya know. She felt sorry for me so she bought me a nice necklace."

Taylor was highly suspicious of Sierra's story, because Sierra used the word Streptococcus.

"Anyway, Taytoe, I have lots of cherishment and emotions for this necklace......lots. So, don't worry about it. It's gonna be fine. Not to mention, even if Fairies were real, they wouldn't know doodlie squat about me or my emotions. Fairies.....phooey."

"Cherishment? Is that a real word?"

"Taytoe.....please, you have got to read more." Sierra brushed her hair away from her face and looked down at Jordan. "What's your peace offering, Jordy?"

"I'm going to use my "Woody" doll. But Tay Tay said I'll get it back. Right?" Jordan looked over at Taylor for confirmation.

"Yes, but we have to leave it overnight. I'll go back tomorrow and get it. So, don't worry Jordy. We need to leave it there long enough to break this bad luck thing, overnight should be good enough."

Taylor tried not to let Sierra get the best of her, but there were times like now when she did. Taylor shook her head and glanced over to Sierra's night stand. "Seems like that music box might be a better choice. We can go back tomorrow and get it. It's not like the Fairies are going to take it."

"No freaking way. After tonight, I am never going over there again. It creeps me out going over to a dead person's house anyway, especially a freshly dead person. There could be spirit or ghost remnants still hanging around."

"You mean to tell me you can believe in ghosts but not fairies?" Taylor shook her head. "That makes about as much sense as a pirate dating a ballerina." Taylor chuckled and opened the wax paper revealing the sweets. "Come on, let's eat."

Sierra sat down on the sleeping bag with Taylor and Jordan without so much as a comment, smirk or side glance at the Hello Kitty's on Taylor's sleeping bag. They ate Mrs. Schmidt's goodies, talked, laughed and made fun of Aleah's summer projects and her inability to take a good photo, until Sierra's alarm went off at 11:30.

"Ok, this is it. You got that crappy necklace?" Taylor grabbed the lanterns, handed one to Sierra, then picked up her backpack and threw it over her shoulders.

"Yes, it's in my pocket. And it's not crappy, Taytoe." Sierra pulled out the necklace far enough to show Taylor it was in her pocket.

"Don't ya wanna clean it up a bit?"

"No. Besides, non-existent fairies aren't gonna care. Clean, dirty, straight, mangled, or tangled .....I'm just saying, they ain't gonna give a frog's fat behiney." Sierra took the lantern from Taylor, gently opened her bedroom door and peeked out. All the lights were off except for a bluish glow coming from the living room. "Come on, the coast is clear."

Taylor and Jordan followed Sierra down the hall, tiptoeing quietly past the living room, where Sierra's mom lay fast asleep on the couch, the empty wine glass reflecting the bluish glow from the TV that was still on. When they reached the front door, Taylor's lantern slipped from her hand. It landed on the wood floor with a loud bang, and broke the silence of the house. The sound bounced off the walls and echoed down the hall.

Sierra's eyes got as big as saucers and exaggeratedly mouthed the words without sound. "Oh, My Gosh!"

Taylor cringed and mouthed the word, "SORRY".

They stood like statues, listening to see if they could hear any movements of arousal coming from the where Sierra's mom was. Nothing but the low sounds of mumbled voices coming from the TV. Taylor bent over, carefully picked up her lantern and whispered softly, "Hope it still works," and pushed the on button with her finger. The entire hallway lit up with Hello Kitty light.

Sierra snatched the lantern from Taylor's hands and whispered angrily. "Are you crazy!?"

"I wanted to make sure it still worked. You're the crazy one! I'm not walking down the street at midnight with no light, depending on you to light my way." Taylor whispered back.

"Oh, come on let's go before I change my mind." Sierra slowly opened the front door and they slipped out.

When they arrived at Mrs. Schmidt's mailbox, Aleah was not there. Taylor looked at her watch. "We're a couple of minutes late."

"Yeah, thanks to you." Sierra said as she flipped opened Mrs. Schmidt's black mailbox and peered inside.

"It's not my fault! Besides, you're the one who fiddled around trying to find your shoes...... and stay out of Mrs. Schmidt's mailbox. I think that's illegal anyway."

"What's illegal? I'm checking to see if she has any mail. She's dead, she ain't gonna care."

"That's considered government property and you can't go rummaging around in people's mailboxes like that, even if they're dead."

"Ya know, Taytoe.....sometimes you're no fun at all." Sierra shined her lantern right in Taylor's face.

Taylor held up her hands trying to block the glaring light.

"Get that light out of my face!"

Sierra dropped the lantern down by her side and out of Taylor's face. "What time is it now.....and where's that pokey know-it-all, Aleah?"

Taylor checked the time again. "Ok, we need to head to the backyard, we have exactly five minutes. Come on...... let's hurry."

"What about Aleah? Don't we need her?" Sierra asked, and quickly followed Taylor and Jordan down the side path to the back. "She's the one we're doing all this foolish stuff for anyway."

"No, we're doing it for you and Jordy, remember? Do you want bad luck the rest of your life?"

"No, but I think this is all stupid."

"Come on and quit complaining, we're running out of time. It's almost midnight."

They stopped in front of the Fairy Ring. Taylor looked up at the moon, full and bright. Like a giant, glowing, orangey-yellow ball, it lit up the whole backyard.

Taylor set her lantern and backpack down. Before they left Sierra's house, Taylor had taken Sierra's music box and hid it in her backpack when Sierra went to the bathroom. Taylor had a bad feeling about the necklace Sierra brought, and questioned if it had any value at all to Sierra. Sierra might jeopardize ever removing the curse from her or Jordan, if she didn't play by the rules. Taylor's plan was to leave the backpack with all its contents in the Fairy Ring, so Sierra would never know. Taylor would retrieve it later, along with Jordan's "Woody" doll.

"You got the necklace, right?" Taylor asked.

"Right here." Sierra pulled the balled-up necklace from her pocket, and shook it a time or two. Bits of pocket fuzz and string still clung to the kinked chain as it dangled in front of Taylor.

Taylor looked at her watch one more time. "Ok, it's time."

"But, Aleah's not here yet. Shouldn't we wait?"

"No, Sierra, we can't wait. Do you want this bad luck curse forever?"

"No."

"We have to do it now and do it right, with or without Aleah and her bushed-up hair." Taylor was perturbed with Aleah for not being there. Taylor didn't like all the responsibility falling on her shoulders. What if something went wrong? Aleah would know what to do. After all, she did a report on it, Taylor thought.

"You need to run around the circle....Now!"

"Ok, ok.....which way do I run? I can't remember which way? Something about the way the Sun travels....which way, Taytoe....which way?"

"Sun travels from East to West, so you're gonna run

counter clockwise." Taylor paused and looked to the East. "Wait a minute."

"Counter clockwise? What the heck....which way is that Taytoe?"

Taylor grabbed Sierra by her shoulders, spun her around towards the east and said "I was wrong.....it's clockwise...... Now, run! Nine times, Sierra, start counting!"

"When do I go, Tay Tay?" Jordan stood there in his Power Ranger pajamas and matching bedroom shoes he had insisted on wearing for this adventure.

"You go after Sierra finishes."

A rustling sound came from the side of the house. "Keep running, Sierra, I think I hear Aleah." Taylor looked at Jordan. "You stay right here Jordy, I'll be right back."

"Don't leave me, Taytoe!" Sierra said as she panted around the ring.

"I'll be right back! Keep running!" Taylor walked back up the path. "Aleah? Aleah, is that you?" Taylor waited a minute but there was no answer. It was quiet, except for the sounds of a cricket's chirp. So, she headed back.

"Was it her?" Sierra was down to a slow jog and panted heavily.

"No....it was nothing. How many times have you gone around the ring now?"

"Six times....no wait.....I think this time will be seven."

Sierra stumbled and tripped over her own feet. "Oh God, this is miserable!" Sierra got up and continued running. "I guess you're going to tell me that was the bad luck that tripped me?"

"Probably not, you know how klutzy you can be," Taylor snickered, "Now please tell me, you know exactly how many times you've gone around the ring, Sierra. Is it six or seven?"

"I was wrong, it's eight. I'm almost done.....and we can...." Sierra was slowing down and trying to catch her breath, "go home and get some sleep!.....and I'm not a klutz!"

Taylor and Jordan watched as Sierra ran around the circle one more time. "Ok, that's nine...right?" Taylor wasn't sure if Sierra knew exactly how many times she'd run around, or if she even cared. Taylor wasn't too concerned with Sierra; after all, she was eleven and knew how to count. Jordy, on the other hand, needed Taylor's help and she wanted to make sure he did it right. Being stuck with bad luck the rest of your life would be detrimental. Even for Sierra.

"Yes, finally....nine!" Sierra jumped into the ring, walked over to where Aleah had piled up the pieces of pulverized mushroom and placed the necklace on top. "There ya go..... that should make Aleah happy......and those stupid Fairies." As Sierra turned to step out of the Fairy Ring, she vanished.

Taylor's heart plummeted to her stomach and swam around like a fish in a tank, trying to find a way out. Taylor's brain couldn't catch up with what her eyes had witnessed. "Sierra? ....Sierra?........Is this a joke?"

"Where'd she go, Tay Tay?" Jordan asked and quickly turned to Taylor for an answer.

"I-I....um....don't know. Sierra must be playing a joke."

"Maybe she shouldn't have called the Fairies stupid." Jordan added.

The backyard was empty and quiet, even the chirping crickets were silent. Sierra was gone. The necklace still lay undisturbed, on top of the broken mushroom. Taylor stood under the moonlight, heart pounding and head throbbing, the words of Mrs. Schmidt echoed loudly in her head.

"I vill alvays be here vhen you need me."

Well, she certainly needed her now. Her whole body felt like rubber and she wondered if her legs would hold her up long enough to walk to the back door.

"Jordy, come with me. I need to see if Mrs. Schmidt can help us."

"But she's dead, Tay Tay."

"Ok well, maybe not. Now come on."

"No, I want to stay here and wait for Sierra."

"Alright. But you wait right here and don't go near that Fairy Ring. You hear me?!"

"Yes, I hear you!" Jordan crossed his arms and frowned.

Taylor stepped up to Mrs. Schmidt's back door and

knocked. She put her ear to the door and could hear faint sounds of music and hoped that was a sign Mrs. Schmidt was still up.

She knocked harder and the door pushed open. Taylor stuck her head inside. "Mrs. Schmidt...... Mrs. Schmidt..... you up? It's Taylor."

Taylor stepped inside the kitchen. It was dark and musty. Not like the earlier smells of fresh baked goods and brewed tea. A soft light leaked in from the hallway, spilling into the kitchen entryway enough to light the way. She followed the sounds of the music down the hallway to the living room from where the light was emanating. "Mrs. Schmidt, you still up? Something's happened. I.....I need your help."

The living room was dimly lit by a floor lamp, with fringe hanging from its shade, gently swaying like there was a breeze in the room. But there was no breeze. On a side table sat an antique record player, a Victrola, with a huge speaker shaped like a giant purple morning glory, playing the music of Fur Elise.

Sitting on a small table, beside a wing back chair with fabric worn thin, was a small plate with a half-eaten crumpet covered with strawberry jam. Still steaming was a cup of tea placed neatly beside it. It was as if Mrs. Schmidt had been plucked from her chair without notice.

"Mrs. Schmidt?" Taylor said softly.

Goose bumps tingled across her arms and prickled up her shoulders and neck. Something felt wrong to Taylor. She wanted to get out of there quickly, back to Jordan, and to find Sierra.

She hurried out. When she reached the kitchen, the music stopped. There was the click of a lamp switch and all went dark. Moonlight shone through the kitchen window, lighting the way out and Taylor ran as fast as her shaky legs could take her.

Taylor froze and her heart nearly stopped. Jordan was standing in the middle of the Fairy Ring.

"What in the name of Sam Hill are you doing Jordy? Get outta there! Now!"

"I was looking for Sierra. She was calling out to me."

"Oh, for the love of Pete, get out of there!"

"Pwease......we gotta help Sierra!"

"We will, Jordy, but first get out of there!" Taylor went to snatch him out, being careful not to step inside the ring. The bad luck curse was bad enough, but what if she'd opened a portal, like Mrs. Schmidt had mentioned.

Jordan began to run around inside the ring to avoid being captured by his big sister. "No...no....I want to help Sierra! Don't you hear her calling me?!"

Only silence pierced the air, and Taylor was frightened for Jordan. "We will help her, but first I need you to get out of there. Now please, Jordy grab my hand." Taylor leaned over and held out her hand, making sure her feet didn't cross into the ring. Jordan hesitated for a moment, then reached for her hand. Only an inch before their fingers touched, he disappeared.

10

Into tHE FaiRY Ring WE Go

Taylor was petrified. Her insides were like mush, as if they had been melted down and poured back into her body. She panicked and ran back into the house, hoping Mrs. Schmidt would be there this time after hearing all the commotion outside, and ready to help. Taylor stopped dead in the kitchen. The darkness was so thick it smothered her. The air was stale and musty, as if nothing good had been baked in that kitchen for years. Not even the moonlight penetrated the dusty windows. Her Hello Kitty lantern was far from reach. Confusion and panic swirled in Taylor's head and she questioned her own sanity. Had Mrs. Schmidt ever really been here? If Sierra and Jordy could disappear into thin air, then visiting a ghost certainly wasn't out of the question, Taylor thought.

Too many questions bounced around inside her head, with no answers. She was totally alone. Sierra and Jordan had vanished; Lord only knows where Aleah was. Something scurried across the kitchen floor and made her jump and squeal like a like a little girl….oh wait….she was a little girl. Back out the door she ran.

"Oh what a tangled web we weave……"

She blamed all this on Sierra, if Sierra hadn't stolen her gossip story, none of this would have happened. How could making up a simple story about a Fairy Ring become so disastrous? Even her little brother got caught up in this tangled web. The night air chilled Taylor, and her feet were wet and cold. Tears spilled down her cheeks.

Taylor wiped her face and slapped herself on the cheek. "Get it together, Taylor…..think…..think….think!" She wished more than ever that Aleah were here or anyone for that matter. It was going to be up to her to fix this. The bad luck curse had been only the beginning of this tangled mess. Taylor was now convinced Mrs. Schmidt had not been joking when she talked about the possibility of opening a portal to the Fairy World. Taylor knew she had no other choice but to go into the Fairy Ring and rescue Jordan and Sierra.

She would use one of her Hello Kitty lanterns as a peace offering to go through the portal. It was past midnight, so running around the ring wouldn't work. She thought about Sierra's music box that was still in her backpack. Maybe if Sierra had used that in the first place, none of this would have happened. Taylor grabbed the music box from her backpack and picked up her lantern. She hesitated for a moment at the edge of the Fairy Ring, then stepped in. Nothing happened.

Taylor opened the lid to the music box. The ballerina popped up and the sounds of "Fur Elise" broke the eerie silence.

She felt queasy and all went dark. The wind whipped, blowing her hair in all directions. Taylor was lifted and spun around and around, as if she were in a giant tornado. It was too dark to see, but Taylor could hear the faint sounds of "Fur Elise". She wasn't sure but she thought she screamed the whole time. As quickly as she was snatched from the ground, she was back again, lying face down in the grass. Only, it wasn't the same grass. She was not in Mrs. Schmidt's backyard.

She looked up to a beautiful pink and lavender sky, tall trees with wide trunks, like fat asparagus, towered over her. All the branches bloomed out at the top like a giant umbrella. Thousands of tiny white lights illuminated those branches like a Christmas tree and showered a sprinkling of light down to the ground below. If it weren't for the fear and uncertainty that occupied her mind, Taylor might have appreciated the beauty that surrounded her.

Taylor got up, with the music box still in her hand. She realized she had forgotten to get Jordan's "Woody" doll, maybe it won't be needed, she hoped. It was quiet, maybe a little too quiet, she thought. Jordan and Sierra had to be here too. But where was here?

She called out "Jordy?.....Sierra?.............anyone?" Silence remained.

A dirt pathway stretched down the middle of flowing lavender grass that glistened from the shimmering lights above. The pathway led to a lighted entrance in the woods. Taylor headed down that path, and realized she had no shoes on her feet. The dirt beneath her bare feet was so soft it felt like walking on powdered sugar. She figured her shoes must have come off during the windy ride over.

Taylor called out to Jordan and Sierra again with no response. They couldn't have gone too far, and hopefully, Jordy and Sierra were together. Taylor thought about Aleah, and how others laughed at her for her childish beliefs in Fairies and their world. Even Taylor had snickered behind Aleah's back....but never again.

She made her way down the powdery path, turning back only once when there was a rustling noise behind her. A soft breeze blew past her and left a lingering scent of honeysuckles and sweet grass. High above, clanging wind chimes played their music with the breeze.

Reaching the end of the path, Taylor stood in front of a huge tree trunk. Carved in the middle of that trunk was a rounded top, weathered door, with a huge wrought iron door knocker that hung in the center. A door you might find at the entrance of a Hobbit's home, Taylor thought. But she seriously doubted that Hobbit's lived here. Taylor stretched a hand towards the door knocker but stopped when the rustling was close behind her.

"I wouldn't knock if I were you." A voice, spoke from the woods.

"Who's there?" Taylor spun around quickly. She backed away from the door and glanced over into the shadows of the woods.

"Not unless you like living in a cage."

"Where are you? Show yourself." Taylor continued backing up until she tripped over something and landed right in a bush.

Taylor got all entangled in the bush limbs and struggled to get up.

"Who are you?" Taylor shouted louder as she tried to free herself from the grasping twigs and leaves.

Out from the woods stepped a tall boy with thick sandy brown hair, that looked like it hadn't seen a brush in months, maybe longer.

"What are you doing, you silly girl?" The boy leaned over to help Taylor.

"I'm not silly!" Taylor stuck her hand out.

"Well from my point of view, and I mean that literally, you look mighty silly wallowing around in those bushes." He grabbed Taylor's hand and pulled her up.

Taylor brushed herself off and gave the boy a closer look. His eyes were bright emerald green; a green that would match most anything he wore, a thought she couldn't help but entertain. Eyes that twinkled every time he blinked with the longest eyelashes she had ever seen on a boy, or a girl, for that matter.

"I'm Andrew." He held out his hand to shake hers.

She shook his hand without saying a word.

"And you are?" Andrew was barefoot, wearing clothes worn and torn in places, but clean.

For a moment, she forgot how to form a sentence. She stammered.

"Uh......um......uh..."

What came out was all wrong.... "Tay....Tayter"

"Tayter? Ha! Your name is Tayter?"

"No, I mean, Taylor....my name is Taylor." What was wrong with her? She couldn't even say her own name. Out of habit, she reached up to fiddle with her earring but it wasn't there. Maybe it had come off with her shoes, maybe she hadn't even worn the earrings, she couldn't remember. She nervously swooped her hair behind her ears and pushed her glasses up to her face.

"What are you doing here?" He gently took her hand. "Come over this way, out of the light. You don't want them to see you."

"Who?"

"Anybody other than whom you're looking for, that's who." He led her over inside the edge of the woods. "Ok, now what are you doing here?"

"I came here to get my little brother and my friend back. They got here by accident. Have you seen them?"

"Believe me, if they got here it was no accident."

"It was an accident! They didn't try to get here on purpose. They don't even know where here is."

"You don't step into a Fairy Ring and accidently end up here. There are things, specific things you have to do, and obviously, they did them." Andrew looked around as if he were expecting someone. "And yes, I've seen them."

Taylor's eyes widened, "Where are they? My little brother, poor thing, must be scared to death and he's still in his pajamas. And where, is here anyway?"

"This is the world of Fairies, Stinky Pinks, and such. I happen to be a Fairy, a runaway Fairy, by the way, thank you very much. And your brother and friend are probably in cages right now, awaiting their fate to be decided by Queen Devineous, our leader. We call her Queen D for short."

"Their fate? You're kidding me, right? They're not going

to kill them, are they?"

"Don't be silly, we're Fairies, not pirates. Fairies would never dream of killing a human, we love humans......the good ones, naturally. Are your brother and friend, good ones?"

"Well, my little brother certainly is. Sierra, on the other hand, that's debatable."

"Your brother should be ok. He'll probably be auctioned off as a pet. As for your debatably good friend, well.......they may sew wings on her and turn her into a Fairy, or at least try. They've never been successful at turning a human into a Fairy yet, but they're working on it. It usually goes horribly wrong."

"No! They can't do that! My little brother cannot be a pet!! And Sierra, well, she might be mean sometimes, annoying a lot, and steals gossip stories, but even she doesn't deserve that. Come on, really, sew wings on her? I thought Fairies were supposed to be good, with wings and sparkly wands.......and tiny. Why aren't you tiny and flying around with wings and being all sparkly?"

"Guuuurl......what kinda world are you living in?"

"A world where Fairies are tiny, with crystal clear wings, make wishes come true and stuff, and....and fly around in front of castles at Disney holding sparkly magic wands. Oh yeah, and put money under pillows. Good stuff like that, not sewing wings on people or turning them into pets, for Heaven's sake! What kind of world are you living in!? Taylor face flushed with heat.

"Wow, Tayter....can I call you, Tayter?" Andrew gave her a wink so quick she would have missed it had there not been a twinkle in it. "I hate to be the one to tell you, but that is not reality. You've read too many Fairy tale books, girlfriend."

"Well, that's what I know about Fairies and no, you cannot call me, Tayter." Taylor reached up to rub the missing teardrop earring again. A habit she now thought made her look childish and stupid. A habit she decided, was time to break.

Fairies can be good, but Fairies are very strict with their rules, and I for one, think those rules are stupid. That's why I'm down here and not up there in all that "rule abiding" mumbo jumbo." Andrew looked upward at the tree where he first met Taylor. "I've been living down here for close to a year, living by my own rules...Ha!...none! And loving it!"

"Shhh......did you hear that?" Taylor held her hand up to silence Andrew, but he ignored her and kept talking.

"Oh, and by the way I am tiny. And so are you. When you go through the portal, you transform to our size."

Taylor looked herself up and down, not sure if she believed him or not.

"Yeah....I know, it's a puzzle to me too."

"Whatever." Taylor wasn't sure she believed him.

"But, when we cross to your world, we look like small insects with exceptionally large wings. Unless you're wingless like me, then we look like any other human. We don't want you humans recognizing us. You'd probably put us in a jar and shake us silly or something like that. You humans can be a little cruel, ya know?"

"Oh yeah, having wings sewn on your back is less cruel than being put in a jar." Taylor said sarcastically. All she really cared about right now was finding her little brother.

"Well, I beg to differ. At least you could fly away if you had wings. Besides, I'd bet you'd like wings, you humans are always wishing you could fly, am I right or am I right?" A huge smile spread across Andrew's face.

"What's that noise? Do you not hear that?" The sounds of a soft humming off in the distance grew louder.

"Yes, I hear that, Fairies aren't deaf ya know. Let's not lollygag. We don't have much time; we need to get somewhere safer. Follow me."

Taylor followed Andrew through a path into the woods, so well hidden by overgrown grass and bush limbs; you'd never know it was there.

They traveled far back into the woods. The humming sounds grew louder.

"This way quickly." Andrew pushed back heavy bush

limbs that covered an entrance to a cave. Once inside, Andrew took a lantern that hung from the cave wall and shook it vigorously. A soft blue glow brightened inside the lantern, illuminating several feet around them as they made their way down the long dark tunnel.

"Before you even ask, I can see the question all over your face. These are Gleebals. Glow bugs." Andrew held the lantern up and pointed to hundreds of tiny moving, glowing bugs squirming all over each other as one massive glob. "When you agitate them, they light up. Don't ask me why, cause I don't know." Andrew shrugged his shoulders.

Taylor didn't care why. She didn't care about anything right now except for finding her little brother and Sierra. She followed Andrew deeper and deeper into the cave. Taylor felt she had no other choice; he was the only one she knew who could help her find her brother. The humming sounds were getting closer.

"What is that noise? Something's after us, isn't it?"

"It's the S.P. Patrol." Andrew sighed. "I knew it was only a matter of time before they were on the hunt. They can sense any changes in the Fairy World, Sector 1 to be precise."

"What's the S.P. Patrol and Sector 1?" Taylor asked.

"That tree you were about to knock on, is Sector 1, where Fairies live."

"Oh."

"And what's the S.P. Patrol you ask? Well, any invasion of strange or foreign objects, like you for instance, they go on a hunt to seek and find. And they don't stop until they find. They're relentless. Once they capture you, they take you to Queen D to be dealt with."

"Dealt with?" Taylor questioned.

"Yeah, to see if you need wings or not. How quickly we forget."

"I didn't forget.....you didn't explain it right, the first time." Taylor huffed.

"Oh, and by the way, they *are* tiny with crystal clear wings and are somewhat sparkly from the pink gas they expel, only they're not Fairies, they're worse. They're Stinky Pinks, S.P. for short. Now come on, not much further and you'll be safe."

"Safe? Are they dangerous?" Taylor questioned nervously.

"It depends on your definition of dangerous. Don't get your hair in a tease, Girlie."

"You're not answering my question. And my hair is not in a teas..." Taylor got cut short when Andrew stopped her at the end of the tunnel.

Andrew reached down, fiddled underneath a pile of leaves and debris, and lifted a door revealing a dark hole in the ground.

"I'll go first and you follow me." Andrew stepped down on a ladder, made from limbs tied together tight by vines.

"You've got to be kidding me? I'm not going down there." Taylor stared down in the deep, dark hole.

"That's fine Tayter, you can stay here and meet the welcoming committee. Just so ya know, they don't take kindly to strangers." Andrew shot her another quick wink.

The humming sounds of the S.P. Patrol echoed off the tunnel walls, they were almost upon them.

"Alright....I'm coming!" Taylor stepped down on the first step. She was still holding on to Sierra's music box, so it made things a little more difficult.

"Grab the hatch and pull it down after you, and be quick about it!" Andrew stepped down further giving Taylor more room.

A bright pinkish glow advanced towards them from the darkness as the humming grew louder. Taylor reached for the hatch door and shut it behind her so quickly she lost her footing on the ladder and slipped. She grabbed the ladder with both hands and the music box slipped from her hands, while her feet dangled in the air.

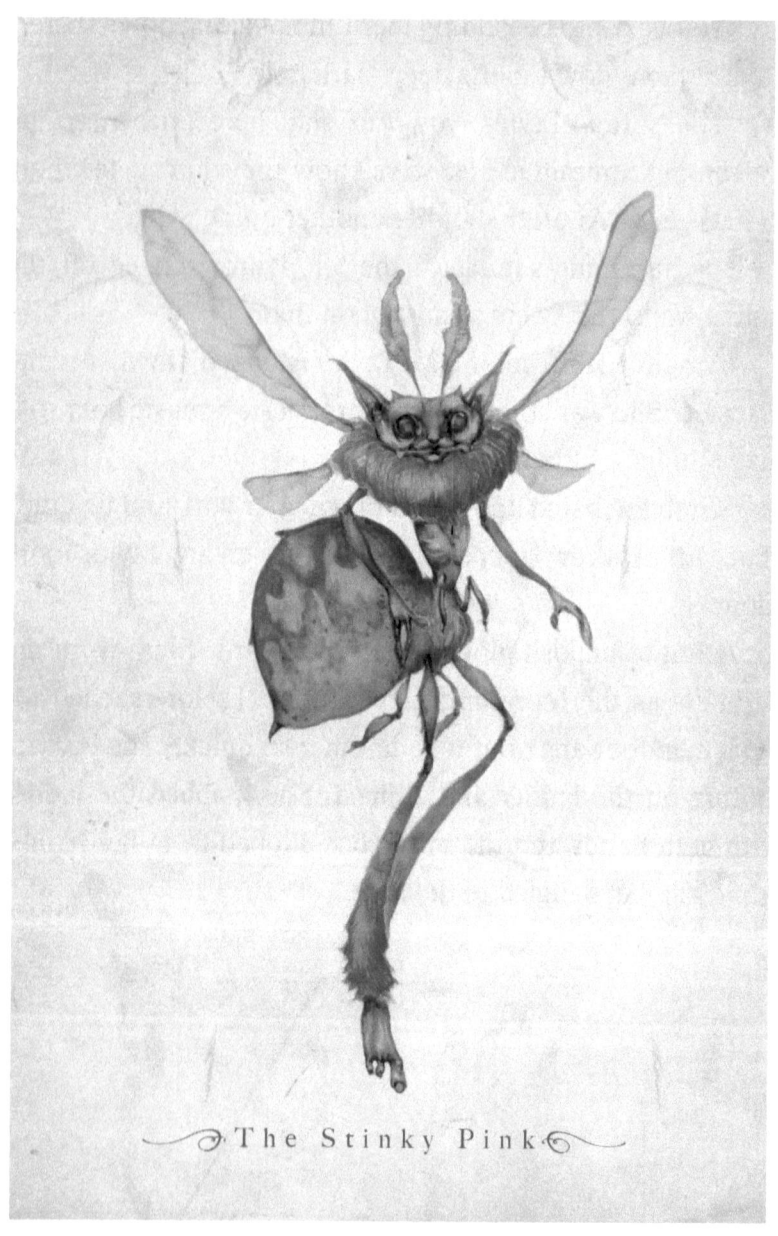

The Stinky Pink

The music box crashed below. A few off-key sounds of Fur Elise trickled out, then stopped with a clunk. "That's just great! Sierra's gonna kill me!"

Andrew grabbed her foot and swung it around to the ladder step. She swung her other foot around, knocking the lantern right out of Andrew's hand.

"Oh no!" Taylor watched the lantern light shrink as it dropped in the darkness below. It landed with a shatter and the massive glob of agitated Gleebals scattered and disappeared.

"Shhhhh.....be quiet. They're right outside the hatch." Andrew whispered.

Taylor held her breath for a few seconds and shut her eyes, afraid they could hear even that. The humming was now a loud buzzing hovering above the hatch. A foul odor seeped down through the cracks of the hatch. Taylor thought she would puke from the smell and put her hand to her mouth. It seemed forever to Taylor, but finally the sounds of the Stinky Pinks faded as they left the tunnel.

"Ok, let's move on down," Andrew said and tapped Taylor on the ankle.

"Sorry about the lantern. What are we gonna do now? I can't see a blasted thing!" And what was that awful smell?"

"They're not called Stinky Pinks for nothing and no worries about the lantern, my clumsy Tayter friend."

"Geez, I said I was sorry." Taylor had not seen his grin

in the dark.

When they reached the bottom, Andrew retrieved another lantern hanging from the cave wall and shook it until the room brightened.

"Come on in, Tayter, nothing to fear here." Andrew walked over to a huge fireplace carved into the wall with a large pipe that led up and out for the smoke to travel. He tossed a few logs onto some dying embers and poked it with a metal rod until the fire began to blaze brightly. The earthy chill of the room began to warm and the room lightened, showing off the home of the wingless, runaway Fairy.

"Welcome to my home."

Taylor noticed a large shelving unit dug out in the wall, full of books of all different colors.

"Wow, you sure do have a lot of books. Looks like a library down here."

"I don't think of them as books."

"Well, they sure look like books to me." Taylor walked over and ran her hand across the backs of a row of books.

"I call them adventures." Andrew boasted.

You actually read?" Taylor hated to read, and only did so when she had to for school. Rarely did she come across a book she enjoyed reading. She thought it was a complete waste of time, especially when there were things like spark notes with condensed versions.

Taylor panned the large room, a typical boy's room, she thought. There were no fluffy throw pillows on the bed, which looked more like a hammock, no mirrors, and no rugs, only the bare necessities. Unlike her room, here everything was neat and in its place, and quite clean for a cave. No television, radio or laptop. No wonder he read.

"Of course, I read. I'm a Fairy, not a pirate."

"That's getting old, I never said you were a pirate."

"Chill, Tayter, I'm reiterating."

"Re what? And would you quit with the Tayter thing, it's Taylor. Taaaylorrrrr."

"Alright.....okay, I'll stop with the Tayter thing, but it sure is fun to watch your eyebrows get all knitted up when I say it."

Taylor reached up and touched her eyebrows without thinking.

"Books are an excellent way to escape the real world. You can go all kinds of places and never step foot outside your door. But I'm sure you know that already. You read much?"

"Yes, I do; in fact, I've read so much it would make your head spin." Taylor said sarcastically.

"Great! Tell me about some of those books. I would love my head to spin."

"Oh, God no, I despise book reports. Now can we please talk about rescuing my little brother?"

"Absolutely, and don't forget your friend......your debatably good friend, what's her name? Siesta? Here Girlie, have a seat." Andrew slid back a handmade, wooden chair from a table which sat in the middle of the room and motioned with his head for her to sit.

"Boy, you sure know how to butcher a name, don't ya. Her name is Sierra."

"Hey, how about a cup of tea? You need to chill and unwind a bit. Shake off some of that Stinky Pink fragrance from your clothes."

"We don't have time for tea. I've got to find my little brother." Taylor grabbed the neck of her shirt and gave it a whiff. "I don't smell anything."

"Ok, girl, if you say so." Andrew waved his hand back and forth in front of his face and crunched up his nose. "Now take a load off." Andrew pointed for Taylor to sit.

Taylor figured she might as well sit, if she was going to get any information out of Andrew. "Jordy is probably scared to death by now. Sierra probably is too, she's not as tough as she puts on."

Andrew poured water from a bucket into a tea kettle hanging on a metal rod and swung it over the blazing fire. He placed two cups on the table and a plate full of over baked cookies, burnt, actually.

"You just figure that out?'

"Figure what out?"

"About your friend Siesta, not so tuff on the inside."

"Yeah, I guess I did, when she showed me her music box last night." Realizing Sierra may never see that music box again made her heart ache, which had never happened before when she thought of Sierra. Deep down Taylor knew it meant much more to Sierra than she had admitted, or probably ever would admit. She couldn't bring herself to look over where it lay broken on the ground. Taylor thought about the broken mushroom Sierra had obliterated and how it could never be fixed, but maybe, just maybe the music box could.

The tea kettle began to whistle with steam and interrupted Taylor's thoughts.

"Anyway, it doesn't matter how tuff she is, I gotta get her out too. I don't have but two friends. I can't afford to lose one. So, you gonna help me or not?

"Most certainly. But first, I need a cup of tea. I need to relax a minute. It helps me think better. Besides, you can't go rushing in there like a Brahma Bull, grab them and leave. You got to have a plan, girl.....a good plan, so you don't get caught."

Andrew removed the tea kettle from the heat. "Now, how about that cup of tea?" Andrew didn't give her time to answer. He put loose leaf tea in an infuser, placed it in Taylor's cup, then poured in hot water.

"So, you're a reader, are you?"

"Did I say that?" Taylor honestly couldn't remember. She only blurted out words to get Andrew to move on and tell her about her brother.

"You sure did Girlie girl."

"Who cares if I read or not? I don't think that's gonna help when we rescue them."

"It might, ya never kno...." Andrew stopped mid-sentence. "What's this "we" stuff?"

"I thought you said you would help me?"

"That part is true, I will help you. But *you,* have to rescue them."

"Ok, whatever. Can we get on with the program? Where did you see them last? Was it near that big tree? Did they go through that door? Did the Stinky Pinks find them?"

"Honey?" Andrew said, looking at Taylor.

"What did you call me?" Taylor felt her cheeks blush with warmth and felt slightly uncomfortable.

"Would you like some honey for your tea?" Andrew placed a jar of golden honey in front of Taylor. "I only have one tea infuser, so I'll be taking that one back." Andrew took the infuser from Taylor's cup and put it in his.

"Oh yeah, sure, I'll give it a try." Taylor chuckled at herself for thinking Andrew had called her honey, and hoped he didn't notice she'd made that mistake. That moment of awkwardness passed quickly. She watched as Andrew made his tea, then he leaned back and appeared to be in no hurry to discuss finding Sierra and Jordan. Nervously she tapped her foot beneath the table.

"How old is your little brother?" Andrew slowly sipped from his cup as the steam crept upward, making his face glisten. And for the first time Taylor thought he looked like a Fairy, all sparkly.

"He's five, nearly six." Finally, Taylor thought, moving forward on the rescue. "And did you say they were in cages?"

"No, I don't think I did." Andrew stirred more honey in his tea, and then licked the spoon clean, getting every bit of honey off.

"So, where did you see them last?"

"Easy now, I'll get to that. But first let's chat a minute. I told you I needed to relax to think." Andrew put his spoon back in the honey jar and ate another spoonful.

"Hey, you don't eat off a spoon somebody else may use," Taylor scolded.

"Why not, I don't have cooties. Are you afraid of cooties? Because I don't have them." Andrew spooned more honey and handed it to Taylor. "Even if I had cooties, you couldn't taste them. Here, give it a lick." Andrew grinned.

"Gross, no thank you." Taylor was getting more and more agitated and wasn't sure how much more of Andrew's stalling she could take. But, she also knew he was right about not rushing in without a plan.

"Why don't you tell me about that music box?" Andrew looked over where the music box lay in the dark, broken.

"It's Sierra's and that's all you need to know!" Taylor didn't feel it was right to tell Andrew about the story behind Sierra's music box and her dad. To Taylor, it would be like revealing the secret of an illusion of Sierra's true feelings. And he didn't deserve to know that.

"I don't see how that's gonna help with the rescue. Can we talk about the rescue please?"

"I think I may be able to fix it before you leave, so you can take it back with you."

Taylor's stomach swirled with nervous butterflies. Clearly, Andrew was avoiding talking about any rescue. All he wanted to do was talk about stupid stuff like books, drink tea and eat honey off a spoon. He had been away far too long from his fellow Fairies. He had too much talk built up in him, that was busting at the seams to come out. He wasn't going to give her what she needed anytime soon. She felt captive.

It was time to think and think quickly, how to get the information she needed from Andrew and get out of there.

11

THE ESCAPE

Taylor did read, even though it wasn't often. She recalled her most favorite book, Coraline. She had read it at least a dozen times. If only there were more books like that, she would certainly be a lover of books.

Coraline had to get needed information as to the whereabouts of her missing parents from an evil "Other Mother". The Other Mother loved to play games. So Coraline played a game with the Other Mother and tricked her in a clever way to get what she needed and found her parents. Taylor loved that part.

An idea popped in her head. Why couldn't she do this with Andrew? He loved books, adventures, and escapes. Taylor devised what she thought was a perfect plan, to get some information out of Andrew.

"So, tell me, Andrew, out of all those books you've read, I mean adventures you've been on, what's your most favorite?" Taylor sipped from her cup and peered up at Andrew, trying to come across as truly interested.

Andrew's eyes lit up like fireworks at Disney World. "Oh....oh by far the adventures of the Robinson Family. They get shipwrecked on an island. They used things they salvaged from the ship and stuff from the island to build a home in the trees. They lived and survived on their own without help from the outside world. And guess what?"

"What?" Taylor leaned closer still faking her interest.

"They eventually ended up living in part of a cave, because Mrs. Robinson hurt herself and couldn't climb up the tree anymore. They lived in a cave, like me! That's the coolest, isn't it?"

"Yeah, that sounds like a book I'd like to read myself." Taylor smiled and nodded at Andrew.

"I've got two relatives, Uncle Demas and Uncle Dermas, who actually live in a tree sort of like that. It's a pretty awesome place, and they don't even have to share it with any of the other Fairies. It's not too far from here. Hey, after you rescue Siesta and the Jordster, we should all go visit them, maybe have dinner. They love company and can cook up a mean Pasta Puttanesca."

"Really? That's pretty cool. Is it like that tree where you found me?"

"Yeah that's right. They actually work as guards in that tree; which are called sectors, even though technically they are trees, Dragon's Blood trees. That's where the Fairies live."

"Pasta Puttanesca, yummy. Yeah, dinner with your Uncles sounds great." Taylor was doing her best to sound sincere and make the conversation last, without rushing and ruining her plan. Taylor's "after rescue" plan didn't include wasting time having dinner with Andrew's Uncles.

"We can eat the pasta, but don't drink the Fairy juice, otherwise you may never want to leave." Andrew laughed so hard, Taylor didn't think he would ever stop.

"Speaking of Pasta Puttanesca, you want to hear a story I read...um.... I mean adventure?"

"Well duh, Girlie girl." Andrew sat up straight and leaned forward across the table.

"It's from a book, "A Bad Beginning" which is the first from a whole series of thirteen books called, A Series of Unfortunate Events. I read them all too." Now that Taylor thought about it, thirteen books was a quite a lot for someone who didn't like to read.

"Go on."

"First, let me ask, is there a certain place they keep prisoners?"

"Only one place....the only place with a red door."

At last some useful information. Taylor thought her plan was working.

"There were these three kids, ya see, whose parents died

in a fire and were sent to live with this terribly awful man, Count Olaf. Their first night, he asked them to make dinner for him. The kitchen was nasty with very little food. They decided to make Pasta Puttanesca, a dish made with very few ingredients, tomatoes, garlic, olives and pasta. There were no pots for cooking, so Violet, she's my favorite, had to scrub out a disgusting spittoon pot and use that. Ever since then, I have always wanted to try Pasta Puttanesca, only not from a spittoon." Taylor smiled, remembering the story and thinking she wouldn't mind reading that book again.

"Well, you don't have to worry about that with my Uncles; they don't even own a spittoon. Even if they did, they certainly wouldn't put your food in it."

"Speaking of your Uncles, what do they guard?" Taylor hoped to keep this game going long enough to get what she needed out of Andrew, without getting impatient.

"Prisoners and such. Between me and you, they're not too good at it."

"Why's that?"

"They sit up there guarding that prisoner door, whilst sneaking sips of fermented Fairy juice, so by the end of their shift they're drunker than a Stinky Pink on a Saturday night."

"Would they be guarding Sierra and Jordy?" Taylor couldn't help it, and felt it was time for Andrew to spill the beans.

Andrew smiled, "Probably" and pushed the plate of burnt cookies closer to Taylor. "You've not tried my cookies, MissTayter. Not even one."

"Quit with the Tayter name! Where's my little brother?!" Taylor lost it, in spite of herself.

"Take a chill pill and eat a cookie. I said "Miss Tayter", not Tayter!" Andrew held up a cookie and grinned.

"Same thing!" Taylor looked at the plate of burnt cookies, with an expression of disgust she'd seen many times on Aleah and Sierra's faces when they looked at her chocolate recipes.

"I want to hear more about this series of thirteen books you read."

"I want to hear more about where my little brother is! Now tell me where he is! You said you would help me!"

"I also told you I needed to relax, and you nagging me right now, is certainly not helping.......just saying." Andrew put another spoonful of honey in his mouth.

"Look, we can talk about books and adventures another time. I gotta find Sierra and Jordy." Taylor was trying to keep calm, but underneath, her blood began to boil. It was becoming obvious to Taylor, that Andrew was in no hurry to give out helpful information.

"Another time? Really? We both know you'll never come back." The smile that had been spread across Andrew's cheeks had fallen from his face. "I'll be thirteen tomorrow."

Andrew pointed over to the wall close to his bed, showing a tick mark for every day he had been down in his cave. "The least you could do is stay and help me celebrate. I don't have a cake, but I do have these delicious cookies." With a half-smile, Andrew shoved the plate of burnt cookies even closer to Taylor.

"Have you lost your ever-loving mind? I need to go!" Taylor wanted to shake Andrew, shake him so hard that the words spilled out and she got her answer. "What a waste of time! You've told me very little that will help me find Sierra and Jordy! And you said you would help me."

"I will help you, Girlie girl. Don't be in such a hurry. It takes days to sew wings on a human, maybe longer for a debatably good human, and auctions for pets are only on Monday's. You got a whole day before auction day."

Taylor realized her plan to get useful information wasn't working fast enough, and she was wasting precious time. She needed to sneak away before Andrew could stop her.

"Ok, I'll tell you more about that book, but first I need another cup of tea please."

"Sure thing, Girlie." Andrew hopped up from his chair, grabbed the infuser and scrounged around for more tea leaves.

This was the opportunity Taylor needed. She tiptoed from the table and before climbing the ladder, Taylor glanced over at Andrew one last time with his head halfway in the cabinet looking for more tea. Taylor felt bad for tricking him. She wished he would come with her. Even though he could be annoying, Taylor liked him.

Taylor climbed the ladder up into the darkness. She was halfway to the top when she felt a hand grab her ankle. She screamed and kicked.

"Please Taylor, stay and talk to me. It gets so lonely down here and you still need a plan."

Taylor looked down at Andrew, barely able to make out his features in the growing darkness. "Come with me then, and help me."

Andrew slowly let go of Taylor's ankle. "I can't go back there."

"Well, be that way! I have to rescue my brother and my Fremesis."

"Your who?"

"Goodbye, Andrew and thanks for the tea and burnt cookies." Taylor pleaded silently in her head for Andrew to change his mind, follow her and be the security she needed right now.

The light that drifted up from Andrew's room grew dimmer as Taylor climbed her way to the top. Unlatching the hook, Taylor opened the trap door and climbed out. She let the door drop.

Before it closed, Andrew hollered, "Goodbye my Tayter

frien….."

The door slammed shut with a loud boom. Then silence and complete darkness surrounded Taylor as she waited for her eyes to adjust. But it didn't help, in fact, Taylor thought it was even darker than before. She thought about her Hello Kitty lantern, her Grandmother, and Mrs. Schmidt and how she needed them all right now. Big tears welled up in Taylor's eyes, it was up to her to figure this out and go rescue Sierra and Jordy. With one hand sliding across the cave wall and the other waving blindly in front of her, she made her way out.

The thoughts of poor little Jordan frightened in a cage kept her focused on her mission of rescue. Allowing for one moment's thought of how scared she was or could she even pull this rescue off, might cripple her courage.

Once outside the cave, she inhaled deeply; the clean air with the scent of honeysuckles refreshed her. Taylor was mesmerized by the tiny lights shimmering high above in the Dragon's Blood tree against a light purple sky. Whilst keeping an eye out for the Stinky Pinks, she walked the path back to the entrance door where she first met Andrew.

Taylor stopped dead in her tracks. Standing by the entrance door reaching for the wrought iron knocker, was Aleah with that familiar camera strapped around her neck.

"Aleah!! Stop!! Don't knock on that door!!"

Aleah spun around quickly and a huge smile spread across

her face. She ran to Taylor and wrapped her arms around her. "Tay! I'm so glad to see you!!"

Taylor felt sure she was the happier one. "Oh my gosh Aleah! I can't believe you're here! What happened to you? Why didn't you meet us?"

"Sorry Tay. Wouldn't ya know my parents decided to stay up late watching a movie, so I couldn't leave on time." Aleah looked around. "Where are Sierra and Jordy?"

"Sierra and Jordy are up there somewhere." Taylor looked up into the depths of the Dragon's Blood tree.

"What the heck happened, Tay?"

"It's such a crazy story Aleah, it's hard for me to believe it myself, and I was there." Taylor gave Aleah a quick account of what had happened up to this point. "So how did you get here with no peace offering?"

"That's a puzzle to me too Tay. When I got to Mrs. Schmidt's backyard, the first thing I saw was your Hello Kitty lantern sitting right in the middle of the Fairy Ring. I heard you calling me for help, so without thinking, I ran right into the ring, got swooped up in a whirl wind and landed here."

"So that's where I left my lantern." Taylor thought for a minute. "That might explain how I got in."

"What do you mean?"

"My Hello Kitty lantern must have been used as a peace offering."

"That still doesn't explain about me."

"No, it doesn't. But we got bigger fish to fry right now."

"Bigger fish?" Aleah looked at Taylor puzzled.

"We gotta find Sierra and Jordy and get the heck outta here."

"How in the world are we going to find them Tay?" Aleah looked up the tree.

"We gotta go up in that tree and look for them. Andrew, the Fairy boy I told you about, said it's called a Dragon's Blood tree."

"Well, that sounds comforting. Dragon's Blood. Yuck."

"Come on, let's peek through that door. My guess, it's our way to the top." Taylor pushed the door open and it creaked on its hinges. Inside was a partially hollowed trunk with a wooden floor, dimly lit by lanterns filled with slowly squirming Gleebals.

"Let's go in." Taylor grabbed Aleah's hand and they stepped inside.

The door quickly shut and the floor began to rise knocking them off balance. Both girls fell to the floor and stayed seated until the lift came to a stop. The door opened.

12

THE Fairy World

A strong wind blew in, swirling Taylor's hair around her face and up in the air. Taylor removed the hair band from her wrist and pulled her hair back. Aleah's wiry bush for hair didn't move.

"Stay right here." Taylor crawled to the edge of the door and peeked out. The air was crisp and cool like the first day of autumn. The shimmering lights she'd seen from below were the lights from individual Fairy homes scattered throughout the tree. The many branches were the pathways that interconnected this Fairy Sector. A beautiful sunset of lavender with streaks of red and orange could be seen through the gaps of the tree leaves.

All was clear. "Come on, Aleah let's go. And watch out for Stinky Pinks."

Both girls stood, still halfway squatting trying not to be seen. It was still light enough to see, but dark enough they could easily hide behind hanging branches and leaves and be well hidden.

"Stinky Pinks? What are those?"

"Tiny flying fairy-looking creatures that poot out the worst smelling gas you've ever smelled in your life, even worse than Sierra's." Taylor snickered under her breath.

Aleah fought the smile that pushed through her face. "That's not very nice, Tay, considering she's not here to defend herself."

"Oh, what's to defend? Sierra would probably agree. In fact, she'd brag about it and want to have a contest." Taylor followed a path to the right. "Come on, this way."

Aleah followed her, constantly looking over both shoulders. "Do you have any ideas where they could be?"

"Keep your eye out for a red door. And just so you know, Aleah, I'm never gonna doubt you again."

"Doubt me about what?"

"Fairies, you dummy."

"I didn't know you ever doubted me." Aleah had a look of hurt growing on her face.

"Well, let's put it this way. I had reservations......profound reservations."

"Profound?"

"Yeah, sorry."

"Isn't that kind of a big word for you Tay?"

Taylor watched a smile creep on Aleah's face and saw a

twinkle in her eye. "Ha! Yes, it is. I'm not even sure what it means, but it sure sounds like I do, uh?" Taylor smiled back.

"Yep, sometimes you surprise me, Tay."

"I am really sorry though. But I've always believed in you Aleah. Never had doubts about you or our friendship. Okay?"

"It's okay, Tay. No one our age believes me either, but I decided I really didn't care. Believing in Fairies always made me happy. And I like being happy, ya know?"

"Yes, I do know, Aleah. Now let's go find that red door."

Off in the distance they watched two Fairies flying together, only inches above the ground, holding a bucket of liquid that sloshed out from side to side as they tried to balance it between them. The girls watched until the Fairies disappeared around a bend.

"What do you reckon's in that bucket, Tay?"

"The wobbly way they're flying, probably fermented Fairy juice." Taylor pondered for a moment. "We might ought to follow them."

"Why's that?"

"Well, those Fairy guards, Demas and Dermas, like to drink Fairy juice."

"Who the heck are they?"

"Andrew's Uncles, come on, let's follow that sloshing bucket."

Taylor and Aleah stayed a safe distance behind them,

darting in and out of hanging branches, remaining out of sight whilst making their way deeper and deeper into the Fairy World.

"Those Fairies are pretty fast, we need to step up the pace." Taylor picked up speed. "Come on Aleah, catch up."

"I'm coming." Aleah caught up with Taylor, but they were falling further and further behind the flying Fairies. Soon the Fairies were out of sight.

They snuck past many Fairy homes, all had a brightly colored door, but none that were red. Most had windows, covered by closed curtains as evening approached.

"How in the world are we going to find Sierra and Jordan? I've not seen a red door yet." Aleah questioned.

"We got to keep looking, and by the way Aleah." Taylor paused for a second.

"Yeah?"

"I don't suppose you have any ideas on how to get us back home once we find Sierra and Jordy, do you?"

"Actually no. There's nothing in any of my Fairy books that I recall, on escaping the Fairy World. It's not even one of those things that comes to mind to look up. Ya know?"

"Yeah, who in their right mind would ever think they'd end up in a Fairy World and need an escape plan."

"Exactly." Aleah agreed.

Taylor and Aleah kept searching down every path,

looking at every door. They even peeped inside a window or two, spying on Fairy families eating dinner or playing board games.

The lavender sky had changed to a hazy purple, soon it'd be dark and Taylor was tired, thirsty and her feet ached, and they had no lantern. When Aleah asked about sitting to rest a minute, Taylor was tempted. But she decided against it, since there wasn't much time before it would be completely dark, and the colors of the doors were already hard enough to see as it was.

She was surprised at how few Fairies she had seen. "I wonder where all the Fairies are? Taylor asked.

"Maybe they turn in early. Good for us though, less likely to be seen." Aleah answered as they trudged on.

"Hey lookie there, Aleah." Taylor pointed over to a door. "What color is that door? Does it look red to you?"

"It's getting so dark, it's hard to tell. Let's get closer."

The two girls snuck up quietly to the door. "I think it's more of a fuchsia color, Tay, take a look."

Taylor's face was inches from the door, when it flung open. Standing in the doorway was a small Fairy girl, who looked to be Jordy's age, with purple hair and a face that looked like she had sprayed glitter all over it. It startled Taylor so, she backed up knocking over a metal bucket that sat beside the door, making a clanging noise so loud it made her ears ring.

Aleah helped Taylor up. "Let's get outta here!"

They ran until they were far from the fuchsia door and the adorable little glitter-faced Fairy. "Wow that was close." Taylor stopped to catch her breath.

"Well, I don't think that was the right door." Aleah said as she panted and puffed.

"Yeah, that would make it too easy."

"What was that......did you hear something?" Aleah paused and looked behind Taylor.

"Yeah, I hear it. Dag nabit! We can't catch a break! Come on we got to go now!!" Taylor heard the familiar humming sounds of Stinky Pinks.

"What is it, Tay?" Aleah hollered as they both picked up speed.

"Stinky Pinks! They must have heard me knock that bucket over.

"I don't know how much longer I can run!" Aleah panted.

"Well, you better find the energy, come on!"

They ran down one path, then quickly darted down another trying to outrun the humming noise that was gaining on them.

Seconds before they were about to be seen by the patrolling Stinky Pinks, Taylor grabbed Aleah by the arm. "This way, quick." Then she pulled Aleah with her, behind a large hanging branch heavy with leaves.

They slid in behind the branch and pressed up against the trunk of the tree. Completely engulfed in leaves, they stood perfectly still.

"Hold your breath when they pass by." Taylor whispered.

"Why?" Aleah questioned.

"Just do it!"

Both girls held their breath as long as they could and listened as the Stinky Pinks buzzed passed leaving a pink trail of smelly gas. When they finally inhaled again, the stench was so horrid Taylor thought she would pass out and looked over at Aleah who had turned a pasty white and looked like she was about to be sick.

"You gonna be ok?" Taylor fanned her hand in front of Aleah trying to get fresh air to her.

"Yes, give me a minute. That smell was horrific! But I have to tell you Tay, that smells nothing like Sierra's poots. I think hers are worse." Aleah snickered and the color flowed back in her face.

"Now that's hilarious, Aleah. Where have you been hiding that sense of humor all your life?" Taylor chuckled.

"I know, right." Aleah said and snorted.

They both laughed so hard, they had tears running down their face. It felt like a release from the exhaustion and tension that had been building up. When they turned to leave, as the stench dissipated, Taylor saw a red door. She hoped and prayed there was only one red door.

"Aleah, look over there. A red door."

"Yeah, that one is definitely red. Red as blood, that one is." Aleah whispered.

"Did you have to say blood?"

"Well…..no, but that's the color it is. It's not really an apple red or a strawber…."

Taylor cut Aleah off. "I get your point. Come on, let's go check it out."

No guards stood watch. An empty stool sat by the door. Hanging from a rusty nail on a branch, was a skeleton key. Taylor grabbed it and quickly shoved it in the key hole.

"You sure about this, Tay?" Aleah was close behind her glancing back over both shoulders.

"Of course not." With a loud click the door unlocked and she pushed the door open enough to peep in.

The room was dimly lit by a dying fire glowing in the fireplace. Dark shadows wavered on the walls from the only two pieces of furniture in the room. A high back wooden chair and a small table were positioned not too far from the fireplace. An unlit candle with only an inch of life left in it and a fancy looking stein with a pointy lid sat on the table.

Over in the far dark corner was a large blanket covering something rather big. Taylor quietly shut the door behind her. The two girls tiptoed into the room. The blanket moved.

"That blanket moved, Tay.....I swear it did." Aleah grabbed tightly to the back of Taylor's shirt and held on.

"Shhhhh." Taylor slowly crept up to the moving blanket, with Aleah still attached to her shirt, reached down, grabbed hold of the corner of the blanket and flung it back.

Taylor and Aleah jumped when Sierra screamed, still holding on to Jordan. Jordan's eyes widened and he leaped from Sierra's hold and into Taylor's arms. "Tay Tay, you found us!" Jordan could hardly talk for crying.

"It's ok Jordy, it's ok." Taylor hugged Jordan so tight and didn't ever want to let him go.

"Thank goodness you guys found us!! They're planning to sew freaking Fairy wings on me. Lord only knows what they want to do with Jordy." Sierra brushed herself off, then she and Aleah joined Taylor and Jordan in a group hug.

An image of Sierra's broken music box, scattered on Andrew's floor, flashed across Taylor's mind. Now was not the time to tell her.

"Okay, we got to figure out what to do next." Taylor looked around the room for anything useful, in case they needed a weapon to ward off Stinky Pinks or guards. Leaning against the fireplace was an iron poker. She grabbed it.

"You don't have a plan already?" Sierra looked crushed.

"No, sorry we don't. We're lucky we got this far." Taylor picked the stein up, pulled back the lid and smelled inside.

"Yuck, smells like rotten fruit. Speaking of rotten, where's the guard?"

"I don't know, last I knew he was on the other side of that door. Maybe he's taking a break." Sierra turned her glare to Aleah. "I thought you knew all about Fairies, Aleah? All that time you spent on that dumb summer project was for nothing."

"It's not possible to know everything about Fairies, Sierra. I'd think you'd be a little more appreciative we're even here. Besides, why is it up to me anyway?"

"Because, out of the three of us, you're the only one that's done any reading about Fairies and Fairy Rings."

"That's not actually true. I've done some reading on Fairy Rings." Taylor admitted.

"You? Really?" Sierra looked at Taylor with disbelief.

"Yes, Sierra really, really."

"Well, you hate to read ya know?"

"I don't need reminding Sierra." Taylor rolled her eyes and continued. "I remember reading if you wear a cap or hat backwards it confuses the Fairies. They won't be able to tell if you're one of them or an intruder."

"That's great, Taylor, that can be useful. Even I didn't know that." Aleah said acting all proud of Taylor.

"I don't suppose you brought any caps with you?" Sierra stared at Taylor with that look of not really expecting an answer.

"Well.....um" Taylor stammered.

"I thought not." Sierra said in disappointment.

"Doesn't matter. We still have to figure out how to get out of here." Taylor said.

"Yeah, you're right, Tay. And you're right too, Aleah, I am glad you're here. Hopefully we won't all end up with wings and can get our little marshmallows outta here....."

"Marshmallows?" Aleah asked puzzled.

"Our butts, Aleah.....our butts." Sierra snickered. "Now back to the guard, if he wasn't there when you came in, maybe he's not there now."

"Yeah, maybe we can walk right out, as easily as we walked in," Taylor said.

"Well there's only one way to find out." Taylor poked her head out of the door, in time to see the guard staggering from out of the bushes and headed back to his guard post. Taylor shut the door.

"The guard is coming back. We'll have to go with plan B."

"What's plan B?" Sierra asked.

"I don't know. I'm making this up as I go along. Give me a minute." Taylor glanced around the room and noticed a small window in the back corner.

"I don't know if we have a minute." Sierra said.

"Come on guys, follow me." Taylor led them to the window and tried to push it open. It was stuck.

"Maybe we can bust it open with that chair." Aleah suggested.

"No, too loud." Taylor took the fireplace poker and pried the window loose, then pushed it all the way up.

"Sierra, you go first, next Jordan. Aleah, you go after him and then me."

They quietly climbed out the window and stood under hanging limbs, out of sight from the guarded door.

"Now what do we do?" Aleah whispered.

The guard sang a song with slow slurred words, and laughed at himself when he'd forgotten the rest of the words.

"Maybe we could make a run for it." Sierra said in a low voice. "I don't think he's in any condition to catch us."

"I wonder if that might be Demas or Dermas?" Taylor peered from behind the limb giving the guard a look over.

"What's a Demas or a Dermas? Sierra questioned.

"Well, I met a boy here and …." Taylor didn't finish before Sierra interrupted.

"I really don't care if it's Tweedle Dee or Tweedle Dum at this point, we need to get out of here and fast, there's a pair of wings somewhere with my name on it!" Sierra snapped.

"Yeah you're right. Let's make a run for it back to the lift where we came in. It's getting darker by the minute. Let's do it. Ready?" Taylor grabbed Jordan's hand.

"Ready," they all said.

The four of them took off, flying past the guard, with hopes they were headed in the right direction. Aleah screamed the whole time with arms stretched out and wavering like a running zombie, startling the guard so; he fell backwards off his stool into the bushes. He got entangled in the limbs and vines as he struggled to get up.

Taylor glanced back at the guard and shocked to see him laughing. She thought it odd, he found humor in his escaping prisoners. Fairy juice must be some good stuff.

They ran until their lungs hurt, only stopping once to catch their breath and figure out where they were, and most importantly, which way the door to the lift was.

"Look, Aleah, there's that fuchsia door where we saw the little Fairy girl." Taylor pointed down a path to the right. "So, we go back that way."

"Great, not much further. Let's run." Aleah said still out of breath.

At last, the door to the lift was in sight. Taylor glanced over at Sierra, who was steadily looking over her shoulders.

"The guard's not coming is he?" Taylor asked.

"No, but I hear something," Sierra said while running and glancing back.

"What does it sound like?" Aleah shouted, glad the door

was in sight because she was running out of steam.

"A buzzing sound."

Taylor and Aleah exchanged glances and said in unison. "Stinky Pinks!"

"What?!" Sierra shouted as she ran.

"Run faster!" Taylor shouted.

They ran as fast as they could and piled into the lift like one connected clump. Once inside, the door began to slowly close. Three flying Stinky Pinks rounded the corner, full speed ahead.

"Shut the door, Taylor!! Hurry!!" Aleah shouted and backed up against the wall.

Sierra grabbed hold of Jordan and held him tight.

"I can't make it shut any faster!" Taylor tried pulling on the door. "For crickey's sake, Aleah help me!!!"

Together they tried to pull the door shut, but it wouldn't go any faster. The Stinky Pinks were so close they could smell their gassy stench, the door shut so fast, it knocked the girls back. Immediately the floor began to move downward. Taylor was exhausted and was thankful for the full two minutes it would take to reach the bottom.

"You reckon those Stinky Pinks have been looking for us the whole-time, Tay?" Aleah asked.

"Oh yeah, they're relentless." Taylor said, and saw the confusion on Sierra's face. "I'll explain it all later, Siesta."

Taylor's mouth pulled into a half smile.

"What did you call me?"

"I said Sierra" Taylor chuckled.

They hit bottom with a jolt and the door opened with the refreshing smell of honeysuckles. They stepped out of the lift and hurried back down the path, not knowing how soon the Stinky Pinks would follow and not knowing exactly where they were going.

13

Sector II

"Now what do we do?" Sierra asked.

"Follow me, I know somebody who might help us." Taylor led them towards Andrew's cave.

Sierra, not paying attention because she was still glancing back over her shoulders, walked right into the back of Taylor when she stopped abruptly.

"Well, well, well. Look at all the Girlie girls.....and this must be Jordy." Andrew stepped out from the bushes.

"And you are?" Sierra asked suspiciously as she looked Andrew over.

"Sierra, this is Andrew." Taylor motioned her hand to Andrew. "Andrew, this is Sierra, Aleah and Jordy."

"Out of curiosity, which one is the Fremesis?" Andrew played ping pong with his eyes looking back and forth between Sierra and Aleah, then glanced at Taylor and grinned.

"A what?" Sierra asked.

"Never mind him, Sierra." Taylor looked back to Andrew. "Andrew, we're in a bit of a pickle." Taylor said feeling slightly uncomfortable to ask for a favor, after the cave incident, but felt she had no other choice and would grovel if needed. "We got Stinky Pinks on our trail, and we have no idea how to get back home. Can you help us get out of here?"

"Oh, now you want my help, uh?"

"Please, Andrew! You gotta help us!"

"Well, I don't gotta, but I will. Follow me." Andrew led them back into the forest near his cave.

"You trust this boy, Taytoe?" Sierra whispered to Taylor.

"Yeah, pretty much. He's a runaway Fairy boy." Taylor mumbled.

"What? He's a what?"

"Shhhh, I think I hear buzzing." Aleah said staying close to Taylor.

Taylor nervously kept a watch over her shoulder, while everyone else watched Andrew as he pulled on a rope that lifted a door hidden by hanging limbs. "Stay here for a minute." Andrew disappeared into the darkness.

The girls and Jordan watched as Andrew backed out of the darkened entryway in a car with no roof. The engine sputtered and the whole car shook with Andrew sitting in the driver's seat. "Come on gang, pile in."

"I'm not getting in that thing. It doesn't look safe." Aleah said as she backed away making room for the ramshackle car.

"Me either, look at it; a disaster on wheels. It looks like a Chitty Chitty Bang Bang reject!" Sierra said, pointing at the metal and wood-framed jalopy that rattled and backfired.

"Your choice, but we've got to get to the next sector, if you want to get out of here."

"I'm in, come on, Jordy." Taylor lifted Jordan in the front seat and climbed in next to Andrew. "Come on girls."

"No way, Tay! That thing can't be safe!" Aleah said shaking her head.

"I'm with Aleah on this one. It's going to fall apart or blow up down the road with us in it!" Sierra said.

They had not heard the buzzing sounds of the fast-approaching Stinky Pinks over the loud sounds of the rattling, roaring jalopy. Taylor looked back and yelled, "Get in now, girls!! The Stinky Pinks are behind you!!"

Sierra and Aleah couldn't get in fast enough and leaped in the back, falling all over each other. Andrew took off fast, knocking the two girls to the floor.

Sierra and Aleah managed to scramble off the floor and climbed to the back seat.

"Where are the seat belts?" Aleah felt around the backseat, but there were none.

"Hang on, Red! We'll be there before you can figure out how to fasten one." Andrew hollered back at Aleah.

"Hey, Fairy Boy! Her name is Aleah, not Red!" Sierra hollered from the back.

Andrew threw up his hand and gave her a thumbs up.

"Can this car outrun Stinky Pinks?" Taylor yelled over the roar of the engine.

"I don't know. Never had to try it before." Andrew smiled and winked at Taylor. "Just so ya know, Stinky Pinks can't go into the next Sector."

"Why's that?!" Taylor looked backed and watched the Stinky Pinks, now shining tiny lanterns in the growing darkness, getting closer and closer.

"They're forbidden to leave their own Sector. They would pop like a balloon if they crossed sectors." Andrew pushed a button on the dashboard and the jalopy's headlights brightened the road ahead of them.

"That's good to know!" Taylor held on tight to Jordan as they sped down the dirt road towards Sector 2 with the Stinky Pinks close behind.

It was a beautiful sight to see all the Sectors scattered across the plain of the Fairy World, like opened umbrellas with thousands of tiny sparkling lights glimmering against a darkening purple sky. Sector 2 was fast approaching.

Taylor watched behind them as the Stinky Pinks slowed and came to a stop. "Are we in the next Sector yet? The Stinky Pinks stopped."

"Yes, we are. We don't have to worry about them anymore," Andrew said as he stomped the pedal to the floor to go even faster, while looking in the rear-view mirror.

"Thank goodness for that!" Taylor said.

"It's the Pigwarts in Sector 2 we have to worry about. They're much worse than Stinky Pinks!" Andrew glanced behind them.

"Don't you mean the Hogwarts?!" Sierra laughed and snorted at her own joke.

"By the way, I figured out which one is your Fremesis." Andrew said with a side glance at Taylor and teasing grin.

"Yeah, not too hard, is it?" Taylor smiled back.

"Fremesis need love too ya know?" Andrew said.

"Yeah, I know, maybe more than others." Taylor answered back.

"Listen up Missy T, all funny business aside. I need you to take the wheel in a minute when we get closer to my Uncle's abode."

"What? Are you kidding me? I've never driven a car before!"

"You don't have a choice. The Pigwarts are right behind us and coming up fast."

"I don't hear any buzzing. Are you sure?" Taylor looked behind her, but saw nothing in the darkness.

"They don't buzz and gas, they're silent, sneaky and shoot darts.....poison darts that are painful and will grow like a wart on your skin." Andrew ducked and dodged as flying darts whizzed passed him.

"What's going on up front?" Sierra hollered.

"You two duck down now! Jordy, you too!" Andrew hollered back.

"It's almost time, Tayter, I'll say when!" Andrew reached under his seat and pulled out a sling shot and a stone.

"Stop calling me Tayt......."

"Ok....Now!!" Andrew leaned out, pulled back on the sling shot and the stone whizzed forward, while Taylor held on to the steering wheel, guiding it with one hand and trying to shield Jordan with the other.

The stone hit metal with a loud "ding" and they all watched as a hidden door opened. Taylor felt a painful burning in her arm as Andrew took over the wheel, slowed down and drove them into the hidden tunnel. The door closed quickly behind them. The room lit up from several hanging Gleebal lanterns.

"My arm! My arm it's burning!" Taylor turned her arm over to see a tiny green dart poking out. She painfully wanted to cry, but didn't because she didn't want to frighten Jordan and didn't want Andrew to think she was weak.

"Quick! Let's go up the lift. My Uncles can help with that. But we gotta hurry before it warts up." Andrew helped Jordan and Taylor out of the jalopy while Sierra and Aleah hopped out of the back.

The Pigwart

"Warts up? What do you mean, warts up?" Taylor winced, holding her arm in pain.

They hurried into the lift and the floor took them upwards.

"You were shot by a Pigwart dart, you silly goose. I told you what would happen. I don't think you're going be very popular back home with warts growing all over your arm. Let's hope one of my Uncles is home." Andrew forced a smile.

"Shouldn't we pull that dart out?" Aleah reached towards Taylor's arm.

"No, not yet, Miss Ginger. It will only make things worse." Andrew held on to Taylor's arm until the lift door opened, then helped her out.

14

THE Uncles

The room was warm and cozy, with overstuffed couches and chairs, begging to be sat on, maybe even slept on, they looked so comfortable. Taylor thought, for two grown Fairy men, who enjoyed maybe a bit too much Fairy juice, the place was immaculate. Everything neat and organized. A blazing fire flickered brightly in the fireplace, a big black cauldron hung over the fire producing a smell of mouth-watering deliciousness that made Taylor realize she was starving, maybe even famished.

"Here, you sit down and stay awake, Girlie." Andrew sat Taylor down on the fluffy couch, put a blanket over her legs and disappeared into the back.

Taylor felt light headed and her stomach queasy. Her eyelids felt heavy. She wanted to rest her eyes until Andrew came back.

"Don't go to sleep, Tay Tay!" Jordan sat down next to

Taylor and shook her slightly.

Taylor winced with pain and the room began to spin. If she could shut her eyes, only for a moment, the spinning might stop.

Andrew and his Uncle entered the room. "Everybody, this is my Uncle Dermas."

They none spoke, but all stared shamelessly. Uncle Dermas wore brightly colored clothes, so bright you had to squint, and a red duster robe that was long and dragged the floor. His hair bushed out like Aleah's only it wasn't red. It was jet black with one white streak that ran smack-dab down the middle, like he had a skunk resting on his head.

"Now which one of you little ragamuffins have a piggydart?" Uncle Dermas smiled and gave the whole lot a look over.

"That would be me." Taylor tried to raise her hand, but only managed a finger.

Uncle Dermas looked down at Jordan with a stern look, and smiled. "Okay little buddy, you need to slide." Jordan quickly moved over and Uncle Dermas sat down next to Taylor.

"Do you need me to get the Dragon's Blood Uncle Dee?" Andrew asked.

"Got it already." Uncle Dermas reached in his robe pocket and rummaged around and stuck his finger through a hole.

"Oh, my….It seems to have fallen out." Uncle Dermas jumped up and searched the floor.

"You better hurry, Unks, I think I see the beginnings of a wart on her arm."

Taylor's eyes widened.

"Come on, Aleah, let's help look," Sierra said and began to look as well.

"What are we looking for, exactly?" Aleah asked, looking under chairs and cushions.

"A small vial of red stuff……ooops….here we go." Uncle Dermas grabbed a small vial from underneath the kitchen table. "Found it."

"Thank God for that," Sierra said sounding relieved.

"I am going to need you to hold her arm and pull the dart out, on the count of three……you ready?"

"Ready."

"One…t…"

"Wait….wait ….wait! That's Dragon's Blood? How sanitary is that? That could cause an infection and her whole arm could rot off!" Aleah said in a panic.

"Easy there, Miss Marmalade. Dragon's Blood is sap from the Dragon's Blood tree; it's thick, sticky and blood red, but not really blood. Ya see, it's completely safe." Uncle Dermas held up the vial for Aleah to see. "It's got healing powers and will seal her wound like a liquid bandage."

"Oh God, the name calling runths in the famiweeee," Taylor slurred, feeling like her lips were melting off her face.

"There's all kinda uses for Dragon's Blood, Missy. Now can we go on before you have a wart for a friend?" Uncle Dermas didn't wait for an answer and continued counting.

When he got to three, Andrew pulled the dart out with one quick jerk and Uncle Dermas dribbled a few drops of Dragon's Blood on the small wound, sealing it immediately.

"That should do the trick. It's also an antiseptic, so that will help with infection. Now who's hungry?" Uncle Dermas got up, went to the kitchen and put a stack of plates on the table. "Ange, you want to give me a hand?"

"Sure, Unks." Andrew replied and helped set the table for seven.

Taylor felt better already and stared at the Dragon's Blood drying on her arm. Her stomach was so empty it felt like it touched her backbone. They were all tired and hungry.

"I'm so hungry I could eat a chicken's butt through a park bench." Sierra said.

"Yuck, Sierra, that's gross." Taylor began to come around and feel like herself again.

"I know, but that's how hungry I am." Sierra laughed.

"Don't you mean a chicken's marshmallows, Sierra?" Jordan giggled.

"Y'all are so disgusting; the chicken's feet are much

tastier." Aleah laughed so hard even her hair shook.

Sierra's eyes widened at Taylor, with a look of shock at Aleah's humor.

"I know, Sierra, Aleah picked up a sense of humor over here. That's funny in itself," Taylor said laughing.

"Why's that so funny?" Sierra continued to laugh.

"I have no idea." Taylor laughed so hard her cheeks hurt.

They were giddy from exhaustion and hunger, but the relief it gave them was what they needed.

Suddenly, the door flung open and in stumbled Uncle Demas. He wore a grayish blue guard uniform and his hair was as bushy as his brother's, only it was all white with a black streak down the middle.

"What we got here?" Uncle Demas said slightly swaying as he stood.

"We got us some stowaways, Demas. We were about to sit down and eat." While the kids scrambled around the table to find a seat, Uncle Dermas set the cauldron on the table along with another pot from off the stove.

"Don't you mean runaways? Those little beasts right there escaped me like Houdini. Knocked me off my stool, they did." Uncle Demas said knitting up his busy black eyebrows.

"They were going to sew wings on me!" Sierra spoke up.

"Yeah, and auction off my little brother as a stupid pet!" Taylor added.

"Is that how you treat visitors? We're all nice people here..." Aleah glanced over at Sierra. "Well, for the most part we are. It's not right!" Aleah chimed in.

"Hold on there, little crumb-snatchers. You're absolutely right. It ain't right! That's why I...um.... let you escape." A huge smile stretched across Uncle Demas's face and then he chuckled loudly.

"What's funny?" Taylor was puzzled.

"I'm always letting the good ones escape. It's not right I tell ya. I'm surprised I still have a job with all the ones I've let get gone." Uncle Demas reached over and ruffled the top of Jordan's hair. "Especially little tykes like you."

Jordan smiled up at Uncle Demas.

"Ok, everyone grab a seat and let's eat!" Uncle Dermas said as he sat down at the head of the table.

"What's in the pots?" Sierra asked, trying to peer in before sitting.

"Pasta and Puttanesca Sauce!" Uncle Dermas said as everyone passed down their plates to be filled. "Every Saturday night it's Pasta Puttanesca!"

"Don't you mean every night, Unks?" Andrew leaned back and laughed so hard he nearly fell out of his chair.

"It's good stuff!" Uncle Dermas said then bellowed out a laugh that shook the whole table. Everyone else joined in the laughter.

As soon as Aleah's plate was filled she took pictures of it, and then snapped a few pictures of the whole gang around the table. No one really noticed as they all began to dig into the delicious meal.

It seemed like such a long time since midnight at the Fairy Ring in Mrs. Schmidt's backyard. Taylor wondered how much longer before they would be back home and safe, or if they ever would. She missed her home, her parents, and Mrs. Schmidt. But for now, the laughter felt good. And she was about to have a wish come true, tasting Pasta Puttanesca for the first time.

Taylor shoveled in a spoonful of Pasta Puttanesca and it was even more delicious than she ever had imagined. No wonder they ate it every night.

Glasses clanged, silverware tinged and all the pasta was eaten. With bellies full and feeling relaxed, the Chocolate Gossip Party girls felt almost normal again, forgetting there was an urgency to leave this place. Everyone but Taylor.

"So, Mr. Dermas, Andrew told us you could help us get back home." Taylor didn't see the need for anymore idle chit chat, and wanted desperately to get everyone back home. Waiting for an answer from Uncle Dermas, Taylor noticed behind him in the kitchen, lined up on the top of the cabinet was a row of odd shaped hats. One had a pointy top that looked like the "sorting hat" from the "Harry Potter" movie;

Taylor thought that would be perfect for Sierra to wear along with her Gryffindor scarf. There was one that especially caught her eye. It was a dark green fedora with a bright red feather stuck on the side.

"Sure, I think we can oblige," Uncle Dermas said, then finished off the last of the Fairy juice from his goblet.

"But, what about your other friends? You're not gonna leave them behind, are you?" Uncle Demas asked Taylor, diverting her attention from the hats and back to the conversation.

"What other friends?" Taylor laughed nervously, and hoped it was a joke. "These are the only friends I have, which are all I can handle, I mean look at the kind of trouble they got me into." Taylor looked at Sierra and Aleah, and smiled before they could take offense, then gave them an awkward wink in case they missed the message in her smile.

"The girls with the long golden hair ain't your friends eh? They arrived shortly after you did." Uncle Demas asked looking a bit puzzled.

"That's right, from the same portal as you's guys came from." Uncle Dermas added. "So, we heard."

Taylor, Sierra and Aleah exchanged glances and Taylor said in a low voice, "The Mansion Girls."

"It couldn't be them. How would they get here? Maybe they overheard our midnight plans?" Aleah was baffled.

Taylor and Aleah stared at Sierra. "Did you tell them about the Fairy Ring plans, Sierra?" Taylor raised an eyebrow at Sierra.

"No! I swear! On a Bible if I had one! I want to keep them as friends. Not scare them away. They'd think I was a pure-T loon if I told them about the Fairy Ring with peace offerings at midnight and such."

"I know what a Loon is, but what does "Pure-T" mean, Senorita?" Andrew asked.

"It means like...um.....like the real thing, or no question about it...something like that, it's just something we say, and my name is Sierra, not Senorita or Siesta or..."

Taylor held up her hand at Sierra. "Give it a break, Sierra, let him call you what he wants, because he will. Believe me, I know. We got to stay focused on getting outta here."

"Alright, Taytoe, but that doesn't mean I have to like it!" Sierra gave in.

"No, Mr. Demas, if it's who I think they are...... they aren't my friends. And I have no intentions of helping them. They can figure it out for themselves, like we are!" Taylor took the last spoonful of pasta, and shoved it in her mouth.

"Well they're my friends, Taytoe and we can't leave them here," Sierra said, slamming down her spoon.

"You save them then! The rest of us are getting outta here!"

"Easy, girls. Let's all take it down a notch. You gotta pass right by where they're being held on the way to the escape portal. What say, you decide when you see 'em, if you's wants to help 'em or not," Uncle Demas said.

"Sure, ok. But I already know the answer to that one." Taylor had no intentions of helping the Mansion Girls. Girls who wouldn't even speak to her, Girls who obliterated her lunch at school one day, Girls who, she was sure, wouldn't help her if the shoe were on the other foot. Even if it were a designer shoe.

"I know they're mean and all, Tay, but between you and me, I don't think they could escape out of a paper bag. I'm just saying...ya know?" Aleah whispered in Taylor's ear.

"Yeah, you're right about that, Aleah. They're as dumb as dirt, no doubt. Probably dumber." Taylor whispered back.

"Ok, first thing to know is, you have to be careful not to be seen. That will be the tricky part. You certainly don't want another piggydart," Uncle Dermas said, then he handed Taylor the vial of Dragon's Blood sap. "Here, take this. One or two drops is all's you need."

"Thanks." Taylor shoved it in her pocket.

"But it's dark, and we should be hard to spot. Right?" Sierra asked.

"The paths are well lit by Gleebal lanterns. You will be hard to miss Girlie girl." Andrew answered.

"Demas here's gonna draw you's a map of the path to follow to the portal hole. Once you's reach the portal, all's you got to do is jump in." Uncle Dermas said.

"Jump in a hole? That's it?" Taylor said.

"That's it. It'll take you right back to the Fairy Ring you rode in on." Uncle Dermas chuckled.

"Ok, listen up, little muskrats and let me tell you about this map." Uncle Demas said after drawing out the map and held it up for them to view.

They all listened as Uncle Demas explained the map, which was brief……very brief. "Ok, all you's got to do is follow the squiggly line from here to there and somewhere in between you will see where the Maniac Girls are being held." Uncle Demas had rolled up the map before any of them got a close look.

"It's actually Mansion Girls, Mr. Demas, but I think Taylor might like Maniac Girls even better." Aleah snickered and poked at Taylor.

Taylor smiled and gave Aleah thumbs up and then turned her attention to the Uncles. "Whose are those?" Taylor pointed to the hats in the kitchen.

"Those would be mine." Uncle Dermas said proudly.

"I was wondering, Mr. Dermas, Sir, if we might borrow a few of your hats?"

"Whatever for?"

"I think they might help disguise us on the way to the portal." Taylor said, still eyeing the hats and thinking if they confused Fairies, they might confuse Pigwarts as well.

"I'm afraid I can't let you do that. Those were a gift from our beloved sister, Determas." Uncle Dermas lowered his head. "And she ain't here no more. Disappeared one day when she was about Andrew's age, before she got her wings. She was all too curious about the human world. We think she found a portal one day and jumped in, and it closed before she could find her way back."

"Or, she liked it there and didn't want to come back." Uncle Demas interrupted.

"We got word not too long ago that she passed away." Uncle Dermas said and lowered his head.

"I'm so sorry about that, Mr. Dermas….and Mr. Demas." Taylor said.

"Well thanks for your sentiment. But ya see, a Fairy never really dies, they only transform into another entity or form. Like a bird, or a butterfly, or maybe a praying mantis, I loves me a praying mantis. Anywho, when that entity dies, they transform into something else, until eventually make full circle back to their original Fairy form." Uncle Dermas said.

"Well maybe you can take comfort in knowing she's not really dead. Right?" Aleah added.

"Well, she's as good as dead to us, cause she ain't here,"

Uncle Demas said and downed a full goblet of Fairy juice.

"Ok, now enough of that, back to the hats, if you's borrow the hats, that means you're gonna give um back. Now how you gonna do that, Missy?" Uncle Dermas said and cocked his head to one side.

"Please, we only need them until we get to the escape hole. We can give them back to you or Andrew before we jump in."

"We ain't gonna be there. You's leaving here on your own." Uncle Dermas replied.

"Well Andrew can go with us. Right, Andrew?"

"Sorry no he can't. This is as far as Andrew can venture in Sector II. He's a runaway remember? He doesn't want to get caught. Besides, if you's get caught, whose gonna be left behind to rescue you? Us, that's who." Uncle Demas said and handed the map to Taylor.

"Well, will you at least see us down the lift?" Taylor asked.

"Of course," the Uncles said in unison.

Aleah took a few more pictures then they all crammed in the lift. The air in the lift felt thick with silence and uncertainty. Taylor was nervous and her mind raced with what to do next. When the door opened they all stepped out.

"Tay Tay, I gotta go to the bathroom." Jordan whispered to Taylor.

"I wish you would've told me before we got in the lift,

Jordy." Taylor was somewhat perturbed.

"Sawwy." Jordan said doing the "I gotta go pee" dance.

"Where's your bathroom?" Taylor didn't wait for an answer. "Never mind, I'll find it. We'll be right back." Back in the lift they went. Taylor found the bathroom for Jordan then waited in the kitchen for him to finish. She stared up at the hats again and pondered for a moment. Then she quickly grabbed four hats, rolled them up, stuffed them around her waistband and covered them up with her shirt. She spread the remaining hats out, so maybe Dermas wouldn't notice right away that the hats were missing. She would figure out a way later to get them back to Uncle Dermas. When Jordan was done they went back down the lift and joined the others.

"Ok, he's good to go now! Y'all ready?" Taylor looked at the other girls.

"No, but let's go anyway." Sierra handed the map back to Taylor.

"Thanks for everything. We appreciate all your help and the delicious Pasta Puttanesca. We'll miss you." Taylor didn't want to come back here with the Stinky Pinks and Pigwarts, but she would like to see Andrew and his Uncles again. And have another bowl or two of Pasta Puttanesca.

15

Down thE Rabbit HolE

They scurried down the pathway, brightly lit by Gleebal lamp posts, as Andrew said it would be, staying close to the edge trying to avoid being seen. Once out of sight of Andrew and his Uncles, Taylor pulled everyone aside out of the lighted pathway.

"Here, put these on." Taylor reached under her shirt and pulled out the hats.

"Taylor May Dawson! You stole those hats!" Aleah's jaw dropped as she took the hat Taylor handed her and examined it. It was a straw hat with a corn cob pipe glued to the side.

"Not too shabby, Tay. You're smarter than I ever gave you credit for," Sierra said and examined the pointed "sorting hat" Taylor handed her. "Purple, my favorite color."

"Sorry, Aleah, I only wanted to borrow them. Desperate times calls for desperate measures ya know. Make sure they're on backwards." Taylor put Jordan's hat on, a cowboy hat, then hers, the dark green fedora with a red feather.

"I want to say, I really liked Andrew's Uncles. But what were their parents thinking when they named them? I mean, Demas, Dermas and Determas. That's hilarious!" Sierra snickered loudly as she tried to figure out which was the front and the back of her hat.

"Stop it, Sierra before someone hears you, especially a Pigwart." Taylor scolded in a hushed voice.

"Well you have to admit, Tay, that is pretty funny." Aleah snickered, and then looked around for any approaching Pigwarts.

"We got more important things to think about right now." Taylor studied the map Uncle Demas had drawn for them.

"This map is practically useless! Look at this!" Taylor held out the map. It had two "x" marks. One showed "you are here", which was the Uncles' home. The other was marked "rabbit hole", with a squiggly line connecting the two.

Out of nowhere, it seemed, two Fairies whizzed by, but then slowed and turned. They headed right in their direction.

"Oh no, Tay, what should we do....run?" Aleah asked nervously.

"No, I think that would make things worse. No better time than now to test the hat trick." Taylor hid the map as they approached.

"What are you youngsters doing out so late?" The Fairy man asked.

"We....we were out playing and didn't realize it was so late. We are headed home right now." Taylor said trying to sound confident in her lie. Even though it was mostly true, they were headed home. At least she hoped.

"Would you like us to follow you home Dearie?" The Fairy lady said.

"Oh, no, we're fine. Thank you very much though... ma'am." Taylor then lowered her voice, "Come on guys let's go." Taylor led them in the opposite direction from where the Fairy couple had been headed.

"Ok, good night then. We will be seeing you all at the Fairy gathering tomorrow, don't forget 12 o'clock sharp." The Fairy couple said and then turned to leave.

"Yeah, that's right....the gathering....12 sharp....um... see ya then." Taylor answered back, doing her best to sound like she knew what they were talking about.

"Wonder what the gathering is all about?" Aleah questioned.

"Probably that thing where they were going to decide what they were going to do with Jordy and me." Sierra answered back.

"Yeah, Sierra, you might be right about that. Thank goodness I "borrowed" these hats, uh, Aleah?" Taylor looked at Aleah then back to the map.

"Yeah, desperate times and all that, Tay, I get it. But, I

hope "borrowed" doesn't turn into "stole". Aleah said.

"Is everything going to be okay, Tay Tay?" Jordan said clinging to his big sister.

"Absolutely, Jordy. I need to figure out which way this wiggly line right here goes." Taylor showed Jordan the line, and studied it for a moment, then looked around. "Ok, according to the map, I believe that's the path over there. See, Jordy, I got it figured out, so don't you worry." Taylor took Jordan's hand and led them down that path.

"How much longer ya think, Tay? I wonder if we're close to where they're keeping the Mansion Gir....I mean Stephanie, Angela and Jennifer. Not that you care," Sierra said.

"You're right, I don't care." Taylor answered nonchalantly.

They all stopped under a lamp post whilst Taylor glanced at the map again. "I think we're getting close. Come on, this way."

"Should we be worried about those Pigwarts, Tay? Ya know they're silent and could sneak up on us and "Wam!" shoot us with one of those wart thingys." Aleah spoke a little too loud for Taylor's comfort.

"Shhhhhh.....Aleah. Are you trying to scare Jordy?" Taylor said in a low voice.

"I'm sorry. I don't want a surprise attack." Aleah said looking all around.

"None of us do, but I think wearing these hats will confuse them and not talking so loud would help too. If it worked on those Fairies maybe it will work for Pigwarts too."

All the Fairy homes were dark, with a porch light on here and there. Except one, up ahead on the right. It was well lit with shadows wavering about inside.

"Hey, look there, I bet that's where they're keeping the Mansion Girls. What cha wanna bet? Let's go see." Taylor led them towards the place with brightly lit windows.

"I thought you didn't want to help them, Tay. I mean, I'm glad we are....I just thought...." Aleah said.

"I don't. I'd like to peek in the window. I would love to see them in their misery. That's not too much to ask for a little retribution, now is it?"

"Why would you want them to be punished, Taytoe? What have they ever done to you? And isn't retribution a big word for you?" Sierra said jokingly.

"That Gryffindor scarf is wrapped around your neck so tight it's cutting off brain function. Did you forget about them squashing my lunch in front of the whole school?" Taylor snapped back.

"They said it was an accident." Sierra said raising her voice.

"That was no accident, Sierra!" Taylor said even louder.

"Shhhhhhh, you two! Do you want us to get caught!"

Aleah said in a low voice.

"Come on then, let's go take a look."

They followed in behind Taylor, single file. Hunched down, they crept to the side window and peered in. There they were....all three, cowering in a corner, the lovely Mansion Girls. Only they didn't look so lovely, as their faces were smeared with dirt, golden hair a tangled mess and the drab clothes they wore looked like they were pulled from a dumpster. Over by a blazing fireplace were three sets of wings, hanging on hooks as if put up there to dry.

"We can't leave them, Tay. Look at those wings. I'm pretty sure those are meant for them." There was a pleading in Sierra's voice.

"Yes, we can," Taylor said. But there was a weakening in her anger only she was aware of. The Mansion Girls, now stripped of their designer clothes, matching jewelry and without every blond hair in place, were unrecognizable. They looked like frightened girls, afraid they may never see home again, not unlike the three girls who stood on the outside looking in. Taylor began to realize, looking at the Mansion Girls, they were really no different than her. They had fears and vulnerabilities, like anyone else; only they hid theirs better, behind mansion walls, designer clothes and painted nails. But there was nothing to hide behind now.

"I wonder why there's no guard, Tay?" Aleah asked.

"Maybe we could simply walk in and get them."

"Maybe they figured out those Mansion Girls were even too dumb to run away." Taylor replied.

"Can't you give them a break?" Sierra pleaded.

"Yeah, like they gave me one." Taylor snapped back. She watched them through the window and could see they had been crying from the tracks left behind on their dirty faces. The feeling of joyful revenge she thought she wanted so much was not there. Taylor felt a strange tug at her heart as she watched them; and fought hard against it, by pulling up the memory of the lunchtime hall scene. But that embarrassment seemed so insignificant now, as they could all very well never make it back home. She could forgive them and move on from it. She was tired of holding resentment and anger for the Mansion Girls, and feeling like she wasn't good enough whenever they were in her presence or even mentioned. Better clothes, better houses, or better anything didn't make them better than her. Not to mention, she'd never stomp on anyone's lunch, unless it was a liverwurst and onion sandwich, and then she might be doing them a favor. Maybe rescuing the Mansion Girls would make things better between them. Maybe, just maybe, they would see her differently too.

"Y'all, stay here. I'm going to check the front door." Taylor snuck around to check the door. It was locked. That would've been too easy, she thought. And nothing had been easy since they got here.

"No good," Taylor said, shaking her head as she walked back. She never officially announced to Sierra and Aleah she had changed her mind to help the Mansion Girls; it went without saying at this point. And she hoped they wouldn't mention it.

"Let's try that window." Taylor and the others pushed with all their might on the window, but it wouldn't budge.

"Oh, it's useless!" Sierra huffed.

"Wait a minute, maybe they can help us. I mean, they gotta be good for something, right?" Taylor half smiled at Sierra and Aleah, then tapped lightly on the window. All three girls inside jumped and jerked their heads around and saw Taylor peering in the window. Recognition flashed across their dirty faces and the smiles that emerged brought about a feeling in Taylor, even she couldn't put it into words. Taylor waved. They immediately jumped up and ran to the window.

"What are you doing here, Taylor?" Jennifer asked in total shock from behind the window.

Taylor turned to Sierra. "She actually knows my name."

"Of course, she knows your name, dummy. It was written all over your sandwich bag they destroyed," Sierra joked with sarcasm.

Taylor ignored Sierra's remark and turned back to Jennifer. "I'm here to rescue you."

"You mean "We"," Sierra added.

"Oh, yes......we," Taylor responded.

The Mansion Girls jumped up and down with relief and excitement.

"Listen, I need you girls to help us lift this window."

"Sure thing." Jennifer reached up and unlocked the window.

Even with the six of them pushing on the window, it still wouldn't budge. "Ok, any ideas on how we can unlock the front door?" Taylor asked.

"No, they locked it from the outside, with a key," Stephanie said, whilst trying to fix her hair in the reflection of the window. "They took all our jewelry, our clothes and shoes and gave us these horrid things to wear. And look at my hair."

"How tragic," Taylor said, not caring that it came out sarcastic and rolled her eyes without thinking. "Right now, we have more important things to worry about. Is there another window in the back we could try?"

"Yes, there's one by the back door," Angela said, cuffing up the sleeves of her "dumpster" shirt to make her look more presentable.

"Back door? There's a back door?" Taylor asked.

"Yes, but it locks from the inside, so we could keep them out, if they tried to come in the back." Stephanie chimed in,

---

with a blank look on her face that made Taylor thankful she had a brain that actually worked.

"What did I tell you about finding their way out of a paper bag, Tay." Aleah said under her breath.

"You couldn't make this stuff up if you tried." Taylor shook her head. "Ok, can somebody go see if you can unlock the backdoor?"

Stephanie ran to the back door and turned the door lock with a click. It was so loud, it could be heard outside the window.

They all cheered. "Shhhhhh, let's keep it down. We've gotten this far, we don't want to be caught now," Taylor said as they all followed her around to the back.

No sooner had Stephanie opened the door when an ear-piercing alarm went off. They all covered their ears. The Mansion Girls stumbled over each trying to get out all at once.

"This way, everybody! Run!" Taylor yelled over the alarm.

Taylor held tight to Jordan's hand as they ran and the rest followed her in the direction to the escape portal.

Lights were coming on everywhere as the loud sounds of the alarm echoed loudly throughout Sector II.

"Where are you taking us, Taylor?" Angela hollered from the back, panting and puffing, and trying to keep her shirt collar from flying up out of place.

"Yeah, Taylor, do you even know where you're going?" Stephanie said.

"Yes, I do know, so keep running!" Which was not a lie, Taylor knew they were going to the escape portal, she just wasn't sure, at this point, if they were headed in the right direction.

"I'm tired, Tay Tay, my legs are hurting and you're squeezing my hand too hard." Jordan said out of breath.

"Sorry, Jordy, a little further, you can make it." Up ahead Taylor could see an odd-looking lamp post, dimly lit, just beyond the path. "I think that's it, come on, this way!"

Shouting and hollering ensued as the Fairies came flying out of their homes and chased after them.

"Get them! They're trying to escape. Release the hounds, release the Cracken!" Taylor thought she heard the Fairies shout.

"What? Did they say release the Cracken?" Taylor shouted not sure if she heard them right.

"No worse, they said release the Pigwarts!" Sierra shouted back.

Taylor's green fedora blew off, but there was no time to stop and get it. By now Uncle Dermas had probably figured out some of his hats were missing. Maybe later he would follow their same path, that stupid squiggly line Uncle Demas had drawn, and find the fedora. She hoped he would.

"They're gaining on us, Tay. What are we going to do?" Aleah shouted.

Taylor put her hand to the Chinaberry necklace around her neck. She had worn it for good luck ever since Mrs. Schmidt had given it to her. Which was exactly what Taylor thought she needed now.

"Sierra, quick, take Jordy's hand and run to that lamp post. I gotta do something, I'll catch up."

All the girls ran past Taylor as she took off her necklace. The crowd of Fairies were closing in. With both hands, Taylor ripped the string that held the necklace together. All the Chinaberries flew into the air like a flock of birds escaping their captor, then fell to the ground and scattered around her. Taylor panicked, the Fairies were so close, she only had time to snatch up three berries from around her feet. Taylor threw the first one at the closest Fairy, who was a big burly Fairy man. As soon as it hit him, he dropped like a two hundred-pound sack of potatoes. Taylor ran faster while looking back and threw another berry.

The berry landed right in the mouth of a Fairy lady who was screaming, "Get her! Get her!". Taylor didn't feel sorry for her, not one bit, when it knocked the Fairy lady backwards taking down three more fairies with her. That's what she gets, Taylor thought. The crowd had not slowed until Taylor threw her last berry.

Taylor tossed it in the air and as it came back down, the Fairies scattered to avoid being hit.

Taylor soon caught up with Sierra and the rest. They were running so fast when they came to the lamp post, they slid to a stop at the edge of a dark and endless hole that lay beneath the light. Stephanie didn't stop in time and slid right into the dark pit. They all stood in shock as Stephanie's body and screams disappeared down into the darkness.

"Oh, no!!" All the girls, screamed, except Taylor.

Taylor stared down into the dark pit. "Well.....somebody had to go first," she said knowing they all had to follow down that same dark hole, but a small part of her was glad that Stephanie probably didn't know that.

"How can you be so heartless, Taytoe? She could be hurt!" Sierra said angrily.

"She's not heartless at all, Sierra. We all gotta go down that hole. Isn't that right, Tay?" Aleah asked peering down the hole.

"Yeah, we sure do, and quickly too, I imagine the Pigwarts, the hounds, and the Cracken, will be here soon" Taylor said half-jokingly, looking over her shoulder.

A layer of thin gray smoke swirled inside the dark hole, as they all stared down into the darkness, wondering who would jump next.

"Is this the right rabbit hole, Tay?" Sierra asked. "I'd hate for us to go down the wrong one.....ya know?"

"Yes, I'm sure of it. Now who wants to go next?" Taylor asked.

The shouts of the angry Fairies were getting louder.

"Come on, we need to jump now." Taylor demanded.

"Wait a minute, hold on. I am not jumping into that hole! Taylor could be wrong....and then what? We're lost forever? And I can't believe they took my Gucci hand bag! Angela said.

"You brought a hand bag?" Taylor asked.

"Yes. Gucci!" Angela responded. "I would like all my stuff baaaaaaa...."

Taylor wasn't being mean or revengeful, at least she told herself that, when she pushed Angela down the hole. There wasn't time to listen to Angela talk about stupid stuff like where's my Gucci hand bag.

"Come on, everybody, we got to jum...." Before Taylor could finish, Jennifer squealed out in pain.

"Ouch! My leg! Something stung my leg!" Jennifer screamed in pain.

"Tay, she's got a piggy dart. You still got that Dragon's Blood?" Sierra said, squatting down to take a look.

"We don't have time to fix that now. We have to go!" Taylor said as flying piggy darts whizzed by them.

"Everybody, jump....Now!" Taylor held onto Jordan tightly and jumped. The rest of the girls followed.

16

Home at Last

Taylor, Jordan, Sierra, Aleah and the Mansion Girls were sprawled out in the middle of the Fairy Ring in Mrs. Schmidt's backyard, dazed. One Hello Kitty light, outside the ring, flickered dimly in the darkness. In the same spot where Sierra had left it, lay the tangled silver necklace with its cheap plastic stone.

"I was afraid I was the only one to make it back," Stephanie said.

"Taylor! You shoved me in!" Angela snapped.

"I did, Angela, but it was more like a gentle push, we had no time to waste. There were angry Fairies and Pigwarts after us." Taylor smiled at Angela who wasn't smiling back.

"Speaking of those "Hogwarts", Tay, you better find that Dragon's Blood for Jennifer." Sierra looked over at Jennifer who still lay on the ground not moving.

"We got to move fast. Jordy bring me the lantern." Taylor retrieved the Dragon's Blood from her pocket as Jordan ran back with the lantern. "Jordy, shine that light on Jennifer's leg. Aleah, I need you to pull the dart out when I say three. Can you do that?"

"Ready on three."

"Is she dead?" Stephanie asked with a trembling voice.

"No, piggy darts don't kill you, they only give you warts, lots of warts." Taylor heard Stephanie and Angela gasp like that might be even worse than death.

"Ok, Aleah, One...two....three!"

Aleah pulled the dart out and Taylor quickly let 2 drops of Dragon's Blood drip to seal the tiny hole. Moments later Jennifer began to come out of her unconsciousness and sat up.

"How ya feeling Jen?" Taylor asked as she quickly put the small bottle of Dragon's Blood sap back in her pocket.

"Oh, you already calling her Jen and you hardly know her?" Sierra said snidely, and flung one end of the gold and maroon scarf over her shoulder.

"Oh, stop Siesta, nobody cares," Taylor answered back.

"I think I'm going to be ok. What was that you put on my leg?" Jennifer said still slightly groggy.

"It'll help it heal. It's like a bandage, so don't wash it off. You let it wear itself off."

"Thank you, Taylor, very much. It feels better already. Can you help me up?"

The Chocolate Gossip Party girls helped Jennifer up as the other two Mansion Girls stood by and watched.

"Jen, you ok? Angela and I need to go before daylight and someone sees us in these horrific clothes," Stephanie said.

"Yeah, I'll be fine, go on. I know my way home," Jennifer answered.

"What were you all doing here so late tonight, Stephanie?" Sierra asked.

"We came to check out this house. We heard it was haunted after that old lady died. We had gotten to the backyard when you all came, so we hid. Then when you all disappeared, we stepped in that thing you call a Fairy Ring, to see if maybe you fell in a hole or something. Next thing we knew, we landed in that weird place, got thrown in that prison and they took our clothes and stuff. They planned to sew wings on us ya know."

"Ok, now listen up everyone. We can't tell anybody about what happened here tonight. No one would believe us anyway."

"You're not the boss of me and I can tell anyone I want." Angela responded.

"Well, go ahead, Angela and then see how fast they put you in the looney bin because they think you're nuts." Taylor snapped back.

Angela's face frowned up and she flung her tangled,

knotted up, golden hair over her shoulder.

Jennifer looked over at Angela with her drab clothing that made her look like an orphan off the streets. "She's got a point, Angela. Look at us, who would believe us now anyway?"

"Ok...whatever! But it's because I decided not to tell, not because you told me!" Angela snapped. "Well we're leaving, Jennifer. We'll see you tomorrow."

Stephanie and Angela left. Their blond hair no longer swayed in rhythm. The other girls and Jordan stood there in Mrs. Schmidt's backyard, still slightly in shock from the whole ordeal.

"Come on, let's get out of here and go home." Taylor grabbed Jordan by the hand to leave.

Something caught Aleah's eye that sparkled in the grass and she bent down to get a closer look.

"Come on, Aleah, don't go back near that Fairy Ring." Sierra watched nervously as Aleah picked up the silver chained necklace and dangled it.

"Wait a minute...." Aleah held the stone up close to her face examining it like a fine jeweler. "This is mine! How did my necklace get here?"

Taylor jerked her head around at Sierra. "Sierra! You said that necklace was yours!"

"Sierra! How did you get my necklace?!"

"I-I…..I'm sorry. I didn't mean to take it." Sierra stuttered. Sierra had hoped that Aleah would not recognize her own necklace all balled up and knotted when she brought it as a peace offering.

"How do you not mean to take something?" Aleah asked.

"I meant to say, I don't know why I took it. It was sometime last year. You showed me the necklace that your dad gave you for no reason at all; it wasn't even your birthday. It didn't seem fair that your dad was still around and mine was gone. And so, I took it. I'm sorry. I don't even like necklaces."

Jordan ran over and wrapped his arms around Sierra's waist. "Blue Guy doesn't have a dad either Sierra, but he has me. And you have me too."

Sierra reached up and wiped the warm tears that trickled down her cheeks, smearing the dirt on her face. She hugged Jordan back and sniffled. "Thank you, Jordy."

Taylor watched as Aleah fiddled with the necklace avoiding eye contact with Sierra. "Maybe it was the necklace that got you in, Aleah."

"Yeah, maybe so, Tay," Aleah said putting the necklace in her pocket. "Doesn't matter, really. If Sierra hadn't brought it, I may not have been able to get in."

"Yep, I believe you're right." Taylor thought about Sierra's music box, the last gift she'd received from her dad. Sierra would probably never see either her dad or the music box ever again. It made Taylor's heart ache.

"I really am sorry, Aleah," Sierra said.

"I forgive you, Sierra."

"Me too, Sierra." Taylor added.

"What did I do to you, Taylor?"

Taylor laughed, "That's for anything you might do in the future."

They all laughed, and together walked out of Mrs. Schmidt's backyard. When they got to the mailbox, Jennifer stopped them.

"Before I go home, I want to say thanks to all of you for rescuing us. I'm sure Stephanie and Angela appreciate it too. It was all so crazy, wasn't it?"

"Yes, it definitely was." Taylor answered, and Sierra and Aleah nodded in agreement.

"Why don't you girls come over tomorrow afternoon and we'll all go horseback riding." Jennifer asked.

"Sure, sounds good to me." Even though Taylor was exhausted, her insides wanted to explode with excitement. She couldn't believe she was going to go horseback riding with one of the Mansion Girls. How quickly things can change, she thought.

They all said their goodbyes to Jennifer and then headed home, with Hello Kitty lighting the way.

17

And tHE WinnER is....?

aylor fought the urge to top her German Chocolate Brownies with a handful of rainbow sprinkles. She went straight by Mrs. Schmidt's recipe, with no deviations. Adding sprinkles wasn't the answer to making her recipe a winner. Not this time anyway.

Jordan sat on a stool at the counter holding Blue Guy in one hand and the frosting spoon in the other. It had been several days since the Fairy Ring incident and Jordan had been accident-free. Taylor assumed the bad luck curse had been broken. "This is the best recipe you've ever made, Tay Tay." He licked all sides of the spoon to get every morsel.

"Thanks, Jordy. I'll be sure and save you one or two after our meeting today." Jordan's face gleamed with excitement. Taylor watched as Jordan licked the spoon clean and thought of Andrew and the honey spoon. She smiled.

The doorbell rang. Jordan hopped off the stool and ran for the door. "Can I let them in, Tay Tay?"

Taylor followed Jordan to the door. "Yep, let them in."

Sierra and Aleah came in both carrying containers holding their chocolate creations. Sierra with her Gryffindor scarf and Aleah with her camera, strapped around her neck, Taylor thought neither one would look right now without them.

"Hey, hey, hey, Jordy!" Sierra reached down while balancing her container in one arm and giving Jordan a hug with the other.

"Hey, Sierra, Blue Guy sure missed you." Jordan blushed and went running off holding Blue Guy up in the air like he was flying.

"He's so sweet and adorable, Tay. Are you sure you weren't adopted?" Sierra laughed jokingly as they headed to the kitchen.

"Very funny, Sierra." Taylor smiled. After learning of Sierra's feelings for her dad and the music box, Taylor was more tolerant of Sierra's snarky remarks. The experience of the Fairy Ring adventure had changed Taylor.

Taylor had a new confidence about her. After all, it was no easy task getting herself, Jordy, a couple of misfit friends and three brainless wonders back home. The hatred she had harbored for the Mansion Girls had dissolved. Stephanie, Angela and Jennifer, were girls with feelings and insecurities just like her, or any other girl for that matter. She felt much better not caring anymore what they thought about her, because she loved herself, and she had two great friends that loved her too. Even though they argued and fussed, they still had fun together. And thanks to their help, she managed to get them out of a harrowing situation and back home.

In the kitchen, Aleah began her ritual of taking photos of three recipes. "I have to admit, Tay, your chocolate recipe looks really good."

Taylor beamed. "Thanks, Aleah." Taylor glanced over all the recipes. "They all look good. I can't wait to dig in."

Sierra leaned over getting a closer look at Taylor's brownies. "Wow, they do look good, Tay. You must've used a real recipe this time. And look, no sprinkles." Sierra's grin spread across her entire face.

"Actually, I did use a real recipe, Sierra."

"Ha! Ya know I'm teasing, Tay. It really does look good. This may be the first time, no wait........this is the first time I'm actually looking forward to tasting your recipe." Sierra calling her Tay had not gone unnoticed, by anyone.

Both Aleah and Taylor laughed, because they knew it was true.

"It's sad but true, Sierra; my recipes have not been the talk of the town, or blog in our case, not in a good way anyway. But, I'm hoping this recipe may change all that. Now let's quit lollygagging and get our gossip on and eat some chocolate."

As they all sat around the kitchen table Sierra steadily took notes for the blog, it was her turn this week, and all their gossip stories today were boring and mundane. Nothing has yet compared to the Fairy Ring story or the story of Mrs. Schmidt's death, who wasn't actually dead, even though Taylor was the only one who knew that.

"It's too bad we couldn't put the Fairy Ring adventure in our blog," Sierra said.

"Even if we did, nobody would believe us," Taylor responded.

"Tru dat, Tayter," Sierra laughed.

"Oh, stop." Taylor snickered.

They sat around the kitchen table tasting all the delicious chocolate concoctions, and wrote down their points, judging for creativity, looks and taste.

"By the way, I wanted to tell you guys the night we got back from the Fairy Ring, I went to remove the film roll from my camera to get it ready to take for developing and it was gone." Aleah told them.

"Are you sure you even had film in there to begin with, Aleah? You know how you can be a scatter brain sometimes," Sierra said in all seriousness.

"She's not a scatter brain, Sierra." Taylor said.

"I might be a little scatter brained sometimes, but not when it comes to my camera. Film was in there! I'm positive!"

"Ok, well what does that mean? You think the Fairies took your film?" Sierra asked.

"Maybe they didn't want that film developed. I would imagine they want their world kept secret from humans, ya know?"

"Who would have taken it though? She had that camera strapped around her neck 24/7." Sierra questioned.

"I only took it off to eat at Andrew's Uncle's house." Aleah remembered.

"Well, there's your answer then. Now I don't feel so bad about taking the hats."

"Two wrongs don't make a right, Tay," Aleah reminded Taylor.

"Yeah, I know, but it's too late now. Hindsight's 50/50," Taylor said.

"You mean 20/20," Aleah corrected her.

"Whatever.....I can't do anything about it now, except hope they find the hats. Nobody had their hats on when we got back home. Maybe they blew off when we jumped and are still there at the portal and Uncle Dermas can find them. I hope."

"Taylor, it's your turn to tally up the points and see who won." Aleah handed Taylor a small calculator she pulled out from her side pocket that she brought to every meeting to make sure there were no mistakes in the calculations.

Taylor took everyone's judging notes over to the counter to calculate in privacy. She carefully added up all the points for each category and did a total. She couldn't believe it; she added the points again and again, to be sure. She had beat them in every category. Taylor had won. She stood there for a minute before announcing it, so she could savor the moment.

"So....who won, Tay? Come on, inquiring minds want to know. Right, Aleah?" Sierra got up from her chair and froze. The sounds of Taylor's dad playing the piano in the living room drifted in the kitchen. "That's ....that's the song from my music box....um....frrr."

"Fur Elise, " Taylor spoke softly. Sadness fell over Sierra's face like a shade being pulled down over a window. Taylor had revealed to Sierra on the walk home that night from Mrs. Schmidt's, how she had taken her music box and how it got broken and left behind. The expression that night of devastation on Sierra's face, was more than Taylor could bear. She wished more than anything she could get it back for Sierra. But there was nothing Taylor could do about that, except to go back to the Fairy World, to Andrew's home and get it.......and she knew that would never happen.

"Ok, everybody, Attention....attention!" Taylor tapped a spoon against a glass. Ting..Ting..Ting. "First place goes to........Sierra!"

Sierra jumped with excitement, "Yay!" Sierra's whole

face lit up, Taylor had never seen her smile so big. Taylor realized winning meant much more to Sierra than for her or Aleah, who still had their dads.

"I was second place and Aleah, you were third."

"I guess we won't be having any more crazy adventures like the Fairy Ring," Aleah said. "Not that I want another one like that."

"Well, there may be one even better," Sierra spoke up.

"What are you talking about?" Taylor asked.

"Jennifer told me about a haunted house, right here in our neighborhood."

"Sounds like another midnight adventure." Aleah sighed. "Nighttime is not good for my picture taking."

"We may need to invite Jennifer to our next Chocolate Gossip Party meeting, Tay," Sierra suggested.

"That would be ok with me. What about you, Aleah?" Out of the three Mansion Girls, Taylor liked Jennifer the best. Taylor thought Jennifer might fit right in with the Chocolate Gossip Party Girls. And she was the only one that thanked them for the rescue. Not to mention, Jennifer had invited them all horseback riding.

"You got my vote. She actually seems pretty nice." Aleah answered.

"Good, I'll invite her for next time. And we'll have to check out that haunted house." Sierra said excitedly and flung one end of her gold and maroon scarf over her shoulder.

"Sounds good to me, now let's eat some more chocolate!" Taylor said, grabbing another brownie.

They laughed and giggled, talked about Pasta Puttanesca, Andrew and his Uncles and how that part of their journey made the risk of getting wings sewn on worth it.

18

THE Return to MRs. Schmidt's

fter Sierra and Aleah went home, Taylor ran over
to see if Mrs. Schmidt was home. She couldn't wait
to tell her the news; she had won the Chocolate
contest using Mrs. Schmidt's delicious recipe. Even though
she'd let Sierra win.

Taylor was looking forward to Mrs. Schmidt teaching her
a new one. Her mouth watered thinking of Mrs. Schmidt's
delicious pastries and goodies. Taylor was especially curious
as to what happened to Mrs. Schmidt the night of the Fairy
Ring fiasco. Mrs. Schmidt had told her she would always
be there when she needed her. But the more Taylor thought
about it, the more she realized she hadn't really needed her
that night, after all. She had figured things out, along with
the help of her friends, a runaway Fairy and a couple of odd
Uncles. But she did need her help for a new recipe.

Taylor's heart dropped to the pit of her stomach when
she got to the front of Mrs. Schmidt's house. The flowers in

the flower boxes were as dead and dried up as they were the night they entered the Fairy Ring. She didn't know if this was a bad sign or the flowers had died naturally, given it had not rained since the day they'd entered the Fairy Ring.

She continued around to the back, hoping Mrs. Schmidt would be standing at the back door, smiling and waving her inside. "Come in and have some tea and pastries," She would say. But it was not to be. The flowers in the back were also dead. The grass was high and hard for Taylor to see the Fairy Ring, but enough to avoid it as she walked up to the back door and knocked.

Taylor peeked in through the window. No lights were on, all was silent as she stood there fogging up the window with her nose pressed up against it. Something on the table caught her eye. It was not delicious pastries, but hats. The very hats she borrowed from Uncle Dermas. All but the green fedora, were laying on top of the kitchen table. Mrs. Schmidt must have found them after they left that night, which was a curious thing, because no one came back home with them on. Maybe they came through after they left, Taylor thought. At least now, she knew where the hats were. Getting them back to the proper owners was the question.

Taylor knocked again, only harder and called out to Mrs. Schmidt. "Mrs. Schmidt, it's Taylor......are you home?" Only silence echoed back. Taylor turned the knob.....it was locked. "Mrs. Schmidt!" she hollered one last time, with no response. Taylor turned and sat down on Mrs. Schmidt's back steps. She had wanted so badly to tell Mrs. Schmidt about winning the contest and the Fairy World adventure. The back-door slowly creaked open. She could smell the aroma of apple pastries before she even turned around. There she stood, in her white apron and faded floral print.

Taylor couldn't get up fast enough. "Oh, Mrs. Schmidt, you're home!" Taylor hugged Mrs. Schmidt so hard, she thought she might turn her into marshmallow cream.

"Oh, my goodness, Sweetness, of course I'm home. Vhere else vould I be?"

"Well, I don't know, but you weren't here the other night."

"You come in and have a seat. Now, how about some hot tea and pastries?" Mrs. Schmidt said and led Taylor to her seat.

"Oh, Mrs. Schmidt, you don't know how good that sounds." Taylor's mouth watered.

Mrs. Schmidt put on the kettle and then put a plate of apple filled pastries on the table. "Are you hungry, Dear?"

"Always for your pastries, Mrs. Schmidt." Taylor's heart warmed and tummy growled. "Oh, and guess what?"

"Vhat's dat, Sweetie."

"I finally won the Chocolate Contest with that recipe you taught me."

"I'm so happy for you. And how did Sierra take the loss?" Mrs. Schmidt placed a cup and saucer in front of Taylor and then poured her tea.

"She took it just fine, because I let her win. She needed to win more than I did. Besides, secretly knowing I won was good enough for me." Taylor smiled. "I hope you'll teach me another recipe, even though I let her win."

"But of course, Lovey." Mrs. Schmidt placed a plate of pastries on the table and a small pitcher of cream. "So, tell me, Sweetie, how are my brudders?"

"What?.....I'm sure I don't know your brothers. I didn't even know you had brothers, Mrs. Schmidt." Taylor thought maybe Mrs. Schmidt was on the beginnings of going senile; she'd been told that happened sometimes to old people.

"I found some of da hats I gave my brudder, Dermas, scattered about in my back yard dis morning, after your night in da Fairy Ring."

"Uncle Dermas is your brother?" Taylor's jaw dropped so low, she thought she'd have to pick it up off the table before she could finish the conversation.

"Yes, and Demas. Day ver alvays such characters. Did tings der own vay, dey did."

"Did you meet my sister? You vould be lucky if you didn't."

"I'm not sure about that, who is she?" Taylor thought

about the Fairy couple that questioned them the night they all escaped.

"Queen Devineous. She vuz alvays da ambitious von. Dat's for sure."

"Oh, good gracious! She's your sister?" Taylor didn't think she could be more surprised than she already was.

"I heard through da Fairy grapevine dat she had a child, a boy. I tink his name is Michael....no vait..... It is Andrew...... Andrew Michael."

Taylor felt like someone had pulled the rug out from under her feet and she was in a free fall, before hitting the ground.....hard. "That means you're a....a....Fair...

"A Fairy, dat's right. A Fairy dat never got her vings, because she ran avay from da Fairy Vorld and hasn't been able to return until now. Now that you've opened up a portal."

"But you've not returned. Why?" Taylor questioned.

"Because, they vill do terrible things to me. Sew vings on me or vorse, make a mockery of me, make me a labor slave for all to see as a deterrent for others thinking of running away."

"But the Queen of Fairy World is your Sister."

"All da more reason they vould. They break no rules Dearie."

Taylor thought of Andrew, and realized now that his mother was Queen Devineous, and maybe that's why he ran away, but said nothing to Mrs. Schmidt. "Maybe you could go for a quick visit; your brothers sure miss you."

"I miss dem too Dearie, but unfortunately not. Once I go through a portal, I can be detected by Stinky Pinks, Pigwarts and other sector protectors."

"Oh, yeah, I'm familiar with those."

"Fairy Rings can be a danger for me. Dat's vhy vhen you leave today, you must close the portal. Only the von who opened it can be the one to close it."

"Sure, tell me what to do."

"Remove each stone, and draw a circle vith your finger vhere it vuz. Den stack dem back under dat mulberry bush, and all vill be as before."

"Ok, that sounds easy enough. I've got to go now, Mrs. Schmidt, but if it's ok with you, I'll come back tomorrow and maybe you can teach me a new recipe."

"Yes, and vee vill have anudder tea party." Mrs. Schmidt wrapped up the remaining pastries and handed them to Taylor.

Taylor removed all the stones, before leaving, and stacked them neatly under the bush.

On the walk home she was so excited, because in a few hours, she, Sierra and Aleah were meeting at Jennifer's house to go horseback riding. Taylor laughed to herself; imagine that, she was going to hang out and ride horses with one of the Mansion Girls. Who would have thought it? Certainly not her. But firstly, she was going to town with her mom and Jordy to the public library and check out a book, an adventure called, "The Swiss Family Robinson." And perhaps best and most unusual of all, she knew now that her neighbor, Mrs. Schmidt, was really Determas, sister of Demas and Dermas, a real Fairy and her friend. And she was not dead, because fairies never really die.

She smiled all the way home. Then a thought occurred to her......had she placed a circle on the ground after each stone she removed?